FAIR WARNING

The *bandito* leader said, "That's a nice horse, *amigo*. Maybe you want to give it to me, *si*?"

"Not in this life," Fargo answered. When the big fellow stepped toward the Ovaro, Skye drew his Colt and shot the two men on his right through the heart. Their leader stopped in mid-stride. "Aw, *amigo* why did you shoot my friends? I wanted to pat your horse, that is all. Now you make me mad."

Fargo aimed between the man's eyes but spoke to the other *bandito* in Spanish. "Drop that rifle and mount up."

The little man obeyed, until he was on his horse. Fargo saw his hand reach for his pistol. The Colt barked once, and the man catapulted over his horse's rump.

Fargo instantly hissed to the sole survivor, "I'm letting you live so you can spread the word that one mean Anglo sonofabitch is on the loose in Mexico."

RIDING THE WESTERN TRAIL

☐ **THE TRAILSMAN #91: CAVE OF DEATH by Jon Sharpe.** An old friend's death has Skye Fargo tracking an ancient Spanish treasure map looking for a golden fortune that's worth its weight in blood. What the map doesn't include is an Indian tribe lusting for scalps and a bunch of white raiders kill-crazy with greed.... (160711—$2.95)

☐ **THE TRAILSMAN #92: DEATH'S CARAVAN by Jon Sharpe.** Gold and glory waited for Skye Fargo if he could make it to Denver with a wagon train of cargo. But first he had to deal with waves of Indian warriors who had turned the plains into a sea of blood. (161114—$2.95)

☐ **THE TRAILSMAN #93: THE TEXAS TRAIN by Jon Sharpe.** Skye Fargo goes full throttle to derail a plot to steamroll the Lone Star State but finds himself with an enticing ice maiden on his hands, a jealous spitfire on his back, and a Mexican army at his heels. Unless he thought fast and shot even faster, Texas would have a new master and he'd have an unmarked grave. (161548—$2.95)

☐ **THE TRAILSMAN #96: BUZZARD'S GAP by Jon Sharpe.** Skye Fargo figured he'd have to earn his pay sheparding two beautiful sisters through a Nebraska wasteland swarming with scalphunting Indians ... but it looked like nothing but gunplay ahead as he also rode upon a clan of twisted killers and rapists called the Bible Boys that were on the hunt for bloody booty and perverse pleasure. (163389—$3.50)

☐ **THE TRAILSMAN #97: QUEENS HIGH BID by Jon Sharpe.** Bullets are wild when Skye Fargo tries to help three enticing beauties find an outlaw who left his brand on them and the Trailsman faces a pack of death dealers in a showdown. (163699—$3.50)

☐ **THE TRAILSMAN #98: DESERT DESPERADOS by Jon Sharpe.** Skye Fargo crosses into Mexico following a stolen statue worth its weight in blood, and stumbles across wagon trains filled with corpses and villages turned into cemeteries. The Trailsman is about to find himself riding straight into a showdown with trigger-happy *banditos* that few would survive. (164083—$3.50)

Buy them at your local bookstore or use this convenient coupon for ordering.

NEW AMERICAN LIBRARY
P.O. Box 999, Bergenfield, New Jersey 07621

Please send me the books I have checked above. I am enclosing $_____
(please add $1.00 to this order to cover postage and handling). Send check or money order—no cash or C.O.D.'s. Prices and numbers are subject to change without notice.

Name_____

Address_____

City _____ State _____ Zip Code _____
Allow 4-6 weeks for delivery.
This offer, prices and numbers are subject to change without notice.

THE TRAILSMAN 98

DESERT DESPERADOES

by
Jon Sharpe

A SIGNET BOOK

NEW AMERICAN LIBRARY

A DIVISION OF PENGUIN BOOKS USA INC.

PUBLISHER'S NOTE

This is a work of fiction. Names, characters, places, and incidents
either are the product of the author's imagination or are used
fictitiously, and any resemblance to actual persons, living or dead,
events, or locales is entirely coincidental.

Copyright © 1990 by Jon Sharpe

The first chapter of this book previously appeared in *Queens High Bid*,
the ninety-seventh book in this series.

SIGNET TRADEMARK REG. U.S. PAT. OFF. AND FOREIGN COUNTRIES
REGISTERED TRADEMARK—MARCA REGISTRADA
HECHO EN DRESDEN, TN, USA

SIGNET, SIGNET CLASSIC, MENTOR, ONYX, PLUME, MERIDIAN
and NAL BOOKS are published by New American Library,
a division of Penguin Books USA Inc.,
1633 Broadway, New York, New York 10019

First Printing, February, 1990

1 2 3 4 5 6 7 8 9

PRINTED IN THE UNITED STATES OF AMERICA

The Trailsman

Beginnings . . . they bend the tree and they mark
the man. Skye Fargo was born when he was
eighteen. Terror was his midwife, vengeance his
first cry. Killing spawned Skye Fargo, ruthless,
cold-blooded murder. Out of the acrid smoke of
gunpowder still hanging in the air, he rose, cried
out a promise never forgotten.

The Trailsman, they began to call him, all
across the West: searcher, scout, hunter, the man
who could see where others only looked, his
skills for hire but not his soul, the man who lived
each day to the fullest, yet trailed each tomorrow.
Skye Fargo, the Trailsman, the seeker who could
take the wildness of a land and the wanting of a
woman and make them his own.

*July, 1860, on the scorching
New Mexico Territory desert,
where beautiful women and death
lurk in the dusty shadows . . .*

1

The big man astride the magnificent black-and-white pinto had Miss Candy on his mind when the stallion's ears came to attention. The ear movement broke Skye Fargo's reverie of the saucy, voluptuous woman far behind him in Colorado.

He glanced down and somewhat to the right of the Ovaro's head. A mouse darted from a clump of the dry desert grass that dotted the desolate landscape. When it was close to another clump, the mouse halted. The powerful Ovaro's muscles tensed the instant it heard the buzz of vibrating rattles start.

Of its own accord the pinto angled left and gave the coiled rattlesnake and its nocturnal victim extra space.

Unperturbed by the death scene playing out on the sand, Fargo looked at the lowering full moon and the constellations long familiar to him. He heard the mouse begin a squeak that ended abruptly; the diamondback had claimed a meal.

Fargo's gaze shifted to stare across the endless bronze desert floor in this part of the New Mexico Territory. He wanted to complete his journey south before falling victim to another blistering high noon. But he held back the urge to change the stallion's walk to a faster gait and rode on toward the invisible southern horizon.

Moments later he noticed something looming ahead in the distance. Squinting and focusing his lake-blues eyes on the indistinct form, he spurred the pinto to trot.

Drawing closer, he made out the unmistakable outlines of several Conestogas parked in a defensive circle.

Approaching the moon-bathed wagons, he shouted, "Rider coming in!" so a sentry wouldn't mistake him for an Apache and start shooting.

Nobody fired at him. Neither did anyone call back.

Fargo rode to the nearest Conestoga, reined the big Ovaro to a halt, and peered through the back canvas drawn and secured for the night. He could just distinguish the dark forms of two people lying on a makeshift bed. "Anybody home?" he queried. He slapped the wagon with his palm. Neither person moved.

Knowing what he would find, he dismounted and climbed inside. He rolled the man over. A bullet hole in the man's forehead stared at him. Fargo didn't bother to check the woman clad in her nightdress.

He crawled through the wagon and dropped to the sand. Going to the next wagon, he spotted the teams of mules and the horses tethered to stakes a short distance to his left. That told him this massacre had not been the work of the Apaches, who preferred mule meat over all other kinds.

Inside the wagon, he found two adults and a child lying askew on the floorboards. Now he knew the massacre had happened so fast and had been carried out so efficiently that nobody had been able to grab a weapon, much less flee in the night.

He went to another wagon and looked in. A man lay naked on the bedding. His fancy top hat, which seemed a bit out of place in this setting, sat on the floorboards nearby, as though handy for donning the moment he awakened, which he'd never do. The weapon that fired the bullet had been held so close that it left powder burns between the man's eyes.

Fargo checked all of the wagons for a sign of life, but he found everyone dead. They hadn't been dead for long. In two instances he felt blood that wasn't yet congealed around the bullet holes in the men's chests.

He stepped to their camp fire, where a few embers still glowed. His hand touched the large coffeepot hanging from a strand of heavy wire above the fire. The pot felt lukewarm.

Fargo stood and went to the tethered animals and set them free. If they're lucky and don't hang around, he thought, they'll go straight to the nearest supply of water, something Fargo could use himself.

Returning to the wagons, he whistled for the pinto. He removed the lid from a water keg and let the Ovaro drink from it while he drank from another barrel and filled his canteen.

After quenching his thirst, he rummaged about in the wagons until he found food supplies. Fargo feasted on day-old biscuits and strips of dried beef. Back on the ground, he went to the wagon bearing hay and oats and took some of both to his stallion.

While he lingered, the moon went down. Shortly after its disappearance, the less brilliant stars began to fade. He mounted up and rode with the morning star on his left.

Soon the sun, huge and red-orange, seemed to burst over the eastern horizon. Majestic and mighty though the wide arc appeared, Fargo wished it'd waited another hour before beaming down on him and the pinto. The cool desert night would quickly transform into unbridled, searing heat. For that reason he had opted to ride all night.

By the time the fiery arc inched halfway up into the sky, he had noticed a column of wispy black smoke on the southern horizon. He urged the Ovaro to canter and headed straight toward the smoke. Fargo knew it came from his destination, Domingo Village. "What next?" he muttered.

A lone buzzard came literally out of nowhere. It made a wide lazy circle high above the pinto, then flew north. Fargo muttered, "Looks like the scavengers have picked up the scent of death."

As he rode toward the black smoke, he watched its ominous column bend abruptly and spread to the southwest, obviously caught in a current of fast-moving air. He rode on.

Nearing the border village—some said it was on the U.S. side, others claimed Mexico, and a few had it straddling the line—he noticed peasants laboring in the sun.

As he rode closer, he saw they were busy digging graves. He counted nine already open and waiting. At least ten more were being dug. Passing through the graveyard, he spied a large red olla. A watery gleam covered the exterior. He turned the Ovaro to it and looked inside. Dismounting, he smiled. Fargo cupped his hands and dipped them into the tepid water, then held it to the Ovaro's waiting lips. After quenching the horse's thirst, he gulped several handfuls down his own sun-parched throat.

He mounted again and headed for the opening in the adobe wall that surrounded the village proper. The smoke rose somewhere close behind the old mission.

A funeral procession arrived at the opening at the same time Fargo did. He moved the Ovaro out of the way and stopped to watch the somber passage.

A boy, no more than twelve years old, led the procession. He looked down while slowly swinging a silver censer of smoldering incense on the end of a long silver chain. Behind the boy walked a short, slim priest who wore eyeglasses. The man's skin was a shade lighter than milk-white, in stark contrast to his black robe, the hem of which swept the ground. Fargo began to frown when he noticed the man wore scuffed cowboy boots. The frown deepened when he saw the priest's fingers were busy, working rather clumsily through the much-used long strand of dark, wooden

12

rosary beads he held. Neither the boy nor the priest glanced at Fargo.

Four men bearing the first wood coffin on their shoulders followed the priest through the gateway. Behind them came other men bearing eight more identical coffins. A crowd of black-veiled mourners brought up the rear of the procession.

A shot rang out.

The burial party halted. Before anyone could turn to look around, the air erupted with fierce Apache war cries.

Carbines barked.

Mourners broke ranks and ran for safety inside the wall. The coffins were quickly lowered to the ground. With fear in their eyes, the pallbearers fled through the opening and scattered, each seeking his own safety.

The terrified screams of the women could be heard over the loud, Apache war cries.

Fargo drew his Sharps from its saddle case, spurred the Ovaro through the crowded entrance, and raced to engage the savages.

The narrow dirt street met another, and Fargo swerved left. He then came to an abrupt right turn, took it, and blasted out of the labyrinth into the square. There he reined back hard. The pinto skidded to a halt.

Half-naked Apaches raced helter-skelter onto the square from its far side. Villagers ran before them, screaming, making it virtually impossible for Fargo to shoot.

He charged forward, riding straight for the attackers. He drew his Colt, shot one point-blank, wheeled around, and shot two more.

An Apache caught a woman from behind, threw her to the ground, and raised his tomahawk. Fargo shot him dead.

Four screaming Apaches rushed him. In quick order

the Colt dropped three. He bloodied the fourth man's head with the Sharps' barrel, then paused to reload both weapons. As he did, two Apaches appeared on a rooftop to his left. Fargo shifted in the saddle and shot both with his Colt.

Most of the villagers' screams cáme from the south part of the hamlet. Fargo replaced the two spent bullets in the Colt, then spurred the Ovaro to attack.

As he tore down a narrow dirt street and took a sharp left turn, the screams grew louder. Before him three Apaches held two of the village women captive. Fargo shot two of the savages as he raced in on them, then he leapt from the saddle and engulfed the third Apache in his arms. On the ground he shot the savage in the heart, then ran toward the next set of terrified screams.

An Apache stood on a roof and aimed his carbine at Fargo. Fargo spun out of the way and fired. Hurtling backward with a large bloodstain on his naked chest, the Apache pulled the trigger. The bullet thudded into the adobe wall next to Fargo.

The Trailsman whistled for the Ovaro, mounted up, and reloaded while looking for red targets. Stalking now, he walked the horse up and down the narrow streets, watching the rooflines and glancing behind him now and then. He noted the smoke that came from a wood structure that he presumed was the community storehouse for ears of corn.

The screams had slackened. He believed the Apaches may have retreated, until a shot was fired and a puff of dirt sprang up in front of the Ovaro.

He glanced up, spotted the half-naked rifleman on a roof, and killed the Apache with one shot.

A peasant ran around the far corner, saw Fargo, stumbled, and fell. Fargo rode to him and told the terrified man to get up and get off the street.

Seeing no more of the Indians, Fargo turned the

Ovaro and threaded his way through the labyrinth back to the square.

One of the villagers cowered behind the well in the middle of the town. Fargo shouted to him, "*Amigo*, go up in the bell tower and look around. Tell me if you see any Apaches." The scared man shook his head. Fargo shouted angrily, "Goddammit, I said go!"

The fellow jumped as though prodded and ran to the tower. While the frightened little man was getting in position, Fargo glanced about the area. The crumpled bodies of white-clad villagers and half-naked Apaches were everywhere he looked. Lining the wall on the shady side of the mission were wounded men and women, too many, too fast, he thought, from this fight. At least a dozen newly made wood coffins lay on the ground at the steps of the mission.

"Señor," the man in the bell tower shouted, "the Apaches are running away!" He pointed northeast.

"Good," Fargo muttered. In a loud voice, he said, "All right, you people can come out now. It's safe. The Apaches have left."

A few people appeared at the corners of the streets to peer around them and make sure it was safe before they ventured out onto the open plaza and fully exposed themselves. Fargo turned the Ovaro and went looking for the cantina.

As he rode down a narrow dusty street, a flash of bright light flitted across his eyes. He glanced to his right to see what caused it. A tall brunette stood watching him through the partly opened door of a hovel. She held an open silver compact at her face. A beam of sunlight had apparently reflected off the gleaming lid.

He started to speak and tell her it was safe to come out, but before he could, the woman drew back and shut the door.

2

Entering the cantina, Fargo glanced about. Two women cowered in the dark shadows that consumed a back corner. Neither he nor they spoke as he went behind the bar and helped himself to a bottle of whiskey. After swigging from it, he said, "You don't have to hide any longer. They're gone." When neither of the women answered or moved from the corner, he asked, "Is there a place where I can take a bath?"

"*Sí,*" one replied.

He swilled from the bottle and waited for her to say where. When she didn't, he said, "Get out of that corner. Both of you step out where I can see you."

They came out into the light spilling through the open doorway, then stopped halfway to the bar and faced him. Both women were about the same size, short, slim, and full-figured. To him they looked as though they might be sisters. One appeared a few years younger than the other. He said, "Now one of you can tell me where I'll find the bath."

The younger woman answered, "Out back *señor.* There's a tub under the shade arbor."

Looking at her, he asked, "What's your name? What's her name?"

"I'm Lupita, *señor.* She's my sister, Chachona."

He saw Chachona's elbow nudge her in the side. Lupita volunteered, "I will fill the tub if you wish."

Fargo drank from the bottle before answering, "Please do. I have something to take care of, then I'll be back." He brought the half-empty bottle with him when he came from behind the bar. Going out the door, he added, "Don't make the water too hot."

Outside, he led the Ovaro to the stable, a long, low shed—he'd shot an Apache on its roof. The Indian's head and shoulders hung over the edge of the roof. One arm dangled down, as though reaching for the carbine lying on the ground. Fargo kicked the carbine away, grabbed the man's wrist, and jerked the body to the ground.

Stepping around the dead Apache, he led the Ovaro under the shed to a water trough. While the pinto drank, he put hay out for him to feed on, then cleaned his hooves and made sure his shoes were tight. Satisfied, Fargo patted the stallion's powerful flank, then left.

At the cantina, Chachona stood behind the bar with a shot glass in front of her. As Fargo neared, she reached beneath the counter and produced a fresh bottle of whiskey. She poured, he drank, and as they stood there, their eyes met. Fargo wondered what she was thinking. The woman, he noted, was pretty enough and had been blessed with ample breasts.

"See something you like?" he asked softly.

She poured him another drink. "Your bath is ready. By now the water's probably cold." She handed him the bottle.

He took it and went out back. The wooden vat was extra wide, and beside it stood a small table with a hunk of lye soap and clean towel on top.

The arbor was a three-sided structure with a roof that angled down sharply at the rear. Fargo set the bottle next to the soap, then undressed, but he kept his hat on. Settling down in the cool water, he rested his head on one end, bent his long legs at the knees, and pressed the soles of his feet against the other end. He reached over and grabbed the bottle, sighed mightily, then sipped from the whiskey. As he began to relax, his eyes closed.

They snapped open when the soft hand touched his left shoulder. Lupita smiled down at him ."Sit up," she said, "so I can scrub your back."

Leaning forward, Fargo felt the palm of her hand rub hard across his back.

Lupita murmured, "My, what a strong back. It's so big, *muy fuerte.*" Half the rag came over his shoulder. Before she drew it back, he saw she had not soaped it, and he wondered why. "Now you can lean back," she whispered.

As he did, she scrubbed his chest. Lupita paused to feel his pectoral muscles and his left bicep. When she did, he heard her suck in a tiny breath. Finally she leaned across him to wash his right shoulder and arm. Her right breast dragged over his powerful chest, then mashed against it. She made little grunts, as though reaching across him was uncomfortable. The active nipple aroused Fargo. He felt his erection rise out of the water.

Lupita gasped. She rested on her haunches, letting her eyes travel up and down his body. Her eyes grew large and her breathing quickened.

Lupita dipped a hand below the surface. Fargo felt her fingers try to wrap around his thick base. She gasped softly and cut her eyes to his. Fargo gave a slight nod.

The young woman stood, pulled her thin cotton dress over her head, and flung it aside. Fargo's gaze focused on her massive blue-black triangle, then moved up to her slightly rounded, trembling belly and then to her breasts, which hung proudly and fuller than he had expected. Her erect nipples were quite small and centered perfectly on brown circles about the size of silver dollars.

His left arm went up to her waist and he pulled her into the vat. She clamped her knees to his manliness, opened her mouth, and pressed it to his. Her energetic tongue explored his, searching over the roof of his mouth, probing his inner jaws, and caressing his gums. Satisfied, she pulled back, came up, and guided a nipple between his wet lips.

Fargo took it, along with the brown areolae and as much of the pillowy breast as his mouth would hold.

She immediately began a series of short gasps punctuated with low moans. "Aaah *qué rico, sí, sí, sí* . . . harder, suck harder . . . *por favor*. Aaah . . . Aahyeeiii!"

Her other nipple rubbed over his cheek. He came off the one he was on, fed the other into his mouth, and rocked his head left and right while sucking hard.

"Aaah," she moaned, and pressed her breasts hard against his face and mouth. She gasped through clenched teeth.

Her hand probed under the water, slid over his flat, muscled belly, and found him again. Keeping a tight grip, she moved off him and knelt at his waist with her back to his face, then looked back at him. Her tongue circled her lips, as though asking if he wanted her to proceed.

Fargo nodded.

She bent her open mouth to just above the throbbing crest. Her long black hair fell from her shoulders to her chest, blocking his view. When he felt her hot tongue start licking, he reached down and drew her hair back. As he watched, she tightened her lips and skillfully slipped his foreskin down to get all of the exposed crown in her mouth. Her head bobbed as she gurgled tiny pleasure-filled sounds. The free hand went

19

underneath him to urge him upward so she could take in more of him.

Fargo obliged her.

He felt amazed she could take as much as she did without choking, but all he heard were more, quicker gurgles mixed in with the lengthy deep moans she emitted. Finally, he felt her lips tighten again, then come up slowly, as though she didn't want to leave a job unfinished. She kissed the peak and sat upright.

Fargo grinned at her as she knelt and straddled him at the hips with her back to his face. He noticed she had a lovely unblemished ass, smooth-textured and a beautiful warm brown.

Then he felt her hand guide the pinnacle of his length to her lower lips and spread them. Her body stiffened just before she squatted to force a few inches of penetration. "Oh, oh, *aayyeeii*," she shrieked. "That hurts . . . aaayyeeiiii!"

Fargo noticed it didn't hurt so bad that it kept her from squatting farther down to take in more.

Lupita leaned forward to get relief and a better angle and got hold of his ankles. He grabbed her by the waist, pulled her down, and thrust upward.

"Aaayyeeiiii," she screamed, and tried to rise, but he held her down and thrust again.

She gulped loudly, grabbed the rim of the tub, and shoved backward, powering him into the hilt.

Fargo set a slow rhythmical pace, and she quickly responded. Soon she was pumping furiously, moaning and groaning for him to go faster and deeper. "Oh, oh, that feels good!"

When the velvety inner membrane began squeezing around his full length, Lupita sat straight up, reached behind, and gripped him at the waist and moaned, "Now, *señor*, now . . . please come with me."

Quickening his thrusts, he felt her buttock cheek

muscles relax, then widen so she could capture his full eruption.

He burst in gushes.

She whimpered, "Oh, oh . . . don't stop, *señor*, don't stop . . . please. Fill me . . . fill me, oh, oh . . . aaaaaagh!"

Fargo relaxed and pulled her down to lie with her back on his chest. Her hands came up and curled around his neck. "What brought you to Domingo, *señor*?" she whispered between labored breathings. "How long will you stay?"

"Have to see a man about a horse. But first I needed a bath."

She rolled over, kissed him hungrily on the mouth, face, both ears, and throat, whispering, "Stay with me. I have a bed. I will cook for you, take care of you. *Sí*?"

"We'll see. What about your sister, Chachona? By the way, how old are you?"

She pressed up, smiled, and slid her nipples back and forth over his chest "Why do you ask about her? I can make you happy." She twisted a strand of her hair as she spoke.

He chuckled. "Yes, honey, I know you can. Do you live alone or with her? And you didn't answer my other question."

Through a half-pout, she replied, "I live by myself, but I don't know how old I am. Chachona is four years older than me. But I can make love better than her."

Fargo suspected a touch of sexual competition existed between the sisters. Wonder if the other is as eager and wild as this filly, he thought, but instead he asked, "What the hell happened here? I saw a lot of coffins."

Obviously angry, Lupita left the tub. She slipped on the dress without bothering to towel dry, then knelt beside the tub and answered while soaping the rag. "A gang of Anglos, bad men, rode into Domingo about daybreak and started shooting. I hid under my bed, so I didn't see anything. Chachona said they killed twenty people before they left with the statue. Lean over so I can scrub your beautiful back."

He bent and asked, "Statue? I don't understand."

Scrubbing his back, she explained, "They took the statue of Our Lady of Guadalupe from the mission. Stand up and I'll wash the rest of your handsome body."

Fargo uncoiled and stood. Spreading his feet apart, he reached up and gripped the log rafters to steady himself against her serious scouring. He felt her rub the washrag all over his rump, then drag it down and wash the inside of his thighs.

"I'm looking for a man named Felix Mercier," Fargo said. "Is he here?"

"No," Lupita replied, and washed over his stomach. "You and *Padre* Bonelli are the only white men in Domingo."

Odd, he thought, that she used the priest's last name. Most of the Catholics I know prefer using their priest's first name. But maybe it's different down here. He dismissed the disturbing thought when the soapy rag touched his knees and thighs.

She grasped his manliness and stroked. He let her enjoy herself a minute before he settled back down in the water.

She sighed at the loss, half-shrugged, and asked, "Is this man Mercier why you came to our village?"

He took the rag from her and rinsed it. Moving suds to dip the rag in clear water, he said, "Earlier, I came across a wagon train. All of the people had been massacred. I think Mercier may have been on that wagon train."

"Perhaps, *señor*, but I wouldn't know. This is the

22

first I heard about a wagon train. Do you think the Apaches were responsible for the murders?"

"No. The teams of mules were still there."

He stood for Lupita to rinse him off from a bucket of fresh water, then he stepped from the tub and let her towel him dry until she lingered at his groin. He yanked the towel from her and quickly dried his legs and feet. She held his shirt open for him. Glancing at her, he asked, "Which way did they go?"

"Who?"

Working his arms into the sleeves, he replied, "The bad men."

"I don't know." She handed him his Levi's.

"Chachona didn't tell you?"

"No."

He pulled on his pants, then sat on the table to put on his socks. "Why didn't she tell you where they went?"

Lupita shrugged. "Who cares which way they went?"

Fargo pulled on his boots. "Seems to me that all of you people should. It was your statue. Are you saying it isn't important?"

Her sigh was long and her shoulders sagged. Avoiding his gaze, she admitted, "*Sí, señor*, Our Lady is important. But the Holy Virgin Mother Mary is gone now. There's nothing anybody can do about that. Why are you concerned? Are you going after those men?"

"No." Fargo strapped on his gun belt, adjusted it, and commented, "If you people aren't concerned, I see no reason why I should be. Think you can fix up something for a hungry man to eat?"

Lupita perked up immediately. Through a wide smile she said, "*Sí.* Follow me. You can nap while I prepare a meal."

Chachona watched them pass through the cantina. Fargo noticed Lupita shoot her sister a fast wink, and the woman answered with a slight nod. He got the feeling their swiftly spoken body language dealt with something other than the sexual encounter.

Outside, Lupita led him past the stable to her door, one of several in a low adobe structure. He waited in the doorway while she went inside the darkened room to light a candle. When the room brightened, he stepped inside.

A small bed, hardly more than a cot, stood against a barren wall. A bureau with one drawer missing stood at the center of the back wall, where a small crucifix hung. The other three drawers were partly open. All were full of unfolded garments, several of which spilled over the edges. The candle was set on a small table against the wall across the room from her bed. The only other sticks of furniture in the room were two old straight-backed chairs. A leg of one had been split and wired back together. The floor, of course, was earthen, packed flat and smooth. He saw no cooking facilities.

Lupita came to him, raised on the tips of her toes, curled both slender arms around his neck, and tilted her head, inviting him to kiss her.

"Later," he said, and withdrew her arms. "Go fix me something to eat."

She sighed and walked out mumbling to herself. Fargo took off his hat and collapsed onto the unmade bed. He closed his eyes, and sleep came within seconds.

Half an hour later Fargo's lake-blue eyes opened the instant Lupita's bare foot touched the door to nudge it inward. She stepped to the small table and set the plate of food and eating utensils next to the candle. Picking up the table, she said, "I hope this meets with your approval."

He sat up and swung his legs from the bed.

She put the table down gently between his parted knees, then sat on the earthen floor to watch him eat.

"Not bad," he told her after taking a bite of scrambled eggs loaded with chiles. "Not bad at all. What did you and Chachona talk about while fixing it?"

"Chachona?"

He took another mouthful of the eggs. "Don't lie to me, woman. I saw the two of you eye-talking earlier."

"Oh, that," she murmured. "She asked if I got in the tub of water with you."

"I said don't lie."

"I told her I did. Did I do wrong? Are you not pleased with me?"

Fargo ate the rest of his food without answering. She's lying, he told himself. Chachona told her what and what not to say, and she's sticking to the story. Wiping the plate clean with the remains of a tortilla, he said, "No, you didn't do anything wrong. Yes, you please me." The bit of tortilla disappeared in his mouth.

He moved the table out of the way and pulled off his boots, then his Levi's and shirt. Reclining, he wiggled a finger for her to come to him.

Lupita sprang to her feet. The cotton dress hit the bureau and fell to the floor. She climbed onto the bed and worked his underdrawers down his long powerful legs and off his feet. Lying on top of him, she parted her smooth thighs and squirmed down until her moist lower lips kissed his hardness. Massaging it with her wetness and tense upper thighs, she nibbled on his chest and nipples.

Fargo had her on her hands and knees, and was poised to reenter her, when the door flew open.

Unperturbed by their nakedness or what he'd interrupted, the priest strode into the room and stepped to the bed. Looking down at Fargo's face, the man blurted, "Mister, the people of Domingo thank you for what you did." His right hand shot out to Fargo's, which gripped Lupita's left hip.

25

Fargo let go of his steadying hold on her and shook Father Bonelli's hand.

Lupita sighed disgustedly, fell forward, and left the bed.

"Er, uh, excuse my appearance, Padre, but I wasn't expecting company." Fargo grabbed for an end of the dirty sheet and drew it over his limbering staff. He glanced at Lupita, who had collected her dress and gone to a darker corner to slip it on. Returning his attention to the little priest, he asked, "So, Padre, how many dead do you have for burial?"

Bonelli squatted. Up close Fargo saw the man was older than he'd first estimated. Perhaps it's his drawn face, Fargo told himself, created by this unfortunate mess. As his name implied, Bonelli didn't appear Mexican, nor even Spanish.

A surge of hope flooded Bonelli's tired dark-brown eyes and betrayed his next words. "Will you come with me to the mission? There is something I would like you to see."

"He's busy," Lupita announced from the corner. "Aren't we?" she asked Fargo.

"It'll wait," Fargo replied dryly to her. "Step outside, Padre. I'll be with you in a minute."

The priest rose quickly from his squat, shook Fargo's hand again, then strode through the open doorway.

Lupita hurried to her lover. In a spiteful tone flecked with uneasiness, she spat, "Don't go. Not now. He will talk you into doing things for him. He will work you all night."

Fargo's head shook. "No, honey. I'll get back to you in a little while. Right now I better see what he has to show me. Can't be near as luscious as what you're teasing me with." He pulled on his shirt.

Lupita retreated to the corner to sulk. Sobbing softly, she whimpered, "If you leave, I'll never see you again."

Pulling on his pants, he grinned. "I'll say one thing, *niña*. You're a persistent she-cat. Don't wander off while I'm gone."

Walking outside into the hot sun was the last thing Fargo wanted to do just then. But, what the hell, he thought, I can't refuse a priest in trouble. He strapped on the gun belt and went outside. "Show the way, Padre," he said.

The priest's fast pace implied time was wasting. Coming onto the plaza it seemed to Fargo that almost all the townspeople had assembled there while he was busy dueling with Lupita. "Padre, how many people are there in Domingo?" he asked.

The priest's left hand sliced an arc through the air. "I'm told one hundred and eleven were alive at dawn. Nineteen were killed and fourteen wounded by the gang of Texicans. The Apaches killed six and wounded ten more before you chased them away. I have twenty-five men, women, and children to bury, and about as many to doctor."

Fargo walked beside him through the crowd. Before entering the mission, he saw the bodies of the slain Apache marauders lined up out in the sun. Farther away, the wounded were being tended to in the scant shadow cast by the mission's western wall.

He counted nineteen freshly made wood coffins lined beside the front steps. In the background to his right he heard a saw hard at work and assumed somebody was making the other six.

Glancing past the crowd, he saw two of the mules from the wagon train round a corner and come onto the square. He knew the other mules and the horses were right behind them, headed for the same source of water.

Walking down the aisle in the heavily shadowed sanctuary, Fargo asked, "How many of the Apaches did we get?"

Bonelli snorted. "*We* didn't get any. Your guns killed twelve."

Fargo was genuinely surprised by the man's revelation. "What do you mean by that? Are you saying these people are defenseless? Not one gun?"

The priest nodded as they came to a halt before the long stone altar. "Yes," Bonelli sighed. "It seems the wall is the villager's only means of defense. Mine is a poor flock. Oh, there may be a French saber or two. But rifles or pistols? No, there are none in Domingo. Weapons bring weapons."

Fargo looked at him. "Well," he began softly, "I suggest you get some weapons, because it looks as though you'll damn sure need them. The Texicans might never come back, but you can count on those dead Apaches' brothers returning. When they do, they won't leave until everybody, including you, are stone-dead. *Comprende?*"

"There shall be no weapons in the villagers' hands," the priest answered quietly. In a stronger voice he said, "But I didn't ask you here to discuss death and the instruments of death."

Fargo's gaze followed the man's pointing finger to an oblong-shaped white enclosure. He saw it as a huge egg sawed in half. It stood upright on a raised pedestal behind the altar. So, Fargo mused to himself, why is he showing me that?

Bonelli explained, "At daybreak today a statuette carved from white birch and polished to perfection stood there. The statuette is a replica of the Precious Image, the Most Perfect Virgin Holy Virgin de Guadalupe, which appeared before an Aztec Indian in the year 1527. Now it is gone, stolen by that band of robbers."

Fargo stared at the clamshell and wondered who was crazier, Bonelli, who despised weapons to the point of committing his flock and himself to early graves before taking up one in defense, who worried over a damn wooden statue when he should be outside comforting the wounded and burying the dead—or himself, who pulled back from an eager and willing Lupita to come look at nothing. The thought made him remember what Lupita said. She claimed the piece of birch was important. Fargo's eyes closed and he shook his head.

"Padre, please tell me why you're telling me all this? If you whittled out one statue, you can make another." He started to turn and walk away.

Bonelli's hand shot from his side and grabbed Fargo by an arm. Tugging Fargo back, he explained, "Like the Precious Image, our statuette cannot be duplicated. Both are one-of-a-kind." When Fargo turned and looked back, Bonelli hastened to add, "You see, the statuette is liberally adorned with precious metals and stones. Gold and silver, rubies and emeralds, many diamonds, and jade from the Far East, to name but a few. Not only is the figurine priceless, therefore impossible to reproduce by this extremely poor parish, but it is also a symbol of their faith in Our Lady, and God. Both provides our daily sustenance and protect us. We must have her back."

Now Fargo knew why the priest burst through the door. The priest needed a gun to go after the thieves, only he didn't want to hold the despicable weapon, much less aim it and pull the trigger. How, Fargo asked himself, do I get myself in these situations?

"Tell me, Father Bonelli, other than the two of us, are there any other whites in Domingo?"

"No, not as far as I know. Why do you ask?"

"I came here to meet a man by the name of Felix Mercier."

The priest tensed visibly. Fargo waited a few seconds for the priest to explain why the name "Mercier" caught his attention, as though the mere mention of it revived an old wound. But Bonelli relaxed as fast as he'd stiffened.

Fargo continued. "He's from New Orleans. Never met him personally, only through a letter he sent me. Said he was coming on a wagon train and would meet me in Domingo today. Before sunup, I came across a train of several wagons that had been parked for the night. Everything living except their stock had been massacred. Best as I could tell, nobody survived. I hoped my man had. But now I guess he didn't."

"I'm sorry to hear this tragic news," Bonelli intoned, shaking his head. After a sigh he glanced at Fargo. The priest's face brightened, and in a tone Fargo thought was a shade too cheery, he offered, "My son, God works in mysterious ways. Perhaps it wasn't meant for you to meet Mr. Mercier. Perhaps God brought you here to serve another purpose."

Here it comes, thought Fargo. He's about to twist my tail and God's intentions. Fargo knew he was already in too deep to slink from the man's grasp. He volunteered, "What do you suppose God has in mind?"

"Recover and return Our Lady of Guadalupe . . . perhaps?"

"Perhaps," Fargo echoed with a slight nod. "So, Padre, which way did the bastards go when they left Domingo?"

"Through the south gate, to Mexico. Will you go after them?"

Fargo exhaled the breath he held. "Yes, I suppose so. Now that I'm here, I'll track them down and bring back your statue." He glanced at the enclosure again. "How tall is the statue and what's the weight?"

Bonelli replied, "As you can see, the statuette is about three feet tall. While I've never lifted her, I would imagine she weighs no more than thirty or thirty-five pounds."

Fargo wondered how he would carry it on the pinto,

and how far he would have to chase the culprits. He wondered about a lot of other things too, such as whiskey and women . . .

As he thought on these things, a husky female voice dripping with a deep southern accent warned, "Go and you will die."

3

Father Bonelli and Fargo half-turned to look toward the front of the building. Angry white sunlight brought Bonelli's left hand up to shield his eyes. Fargo squinted into the dust-filled glare.

A woman moved from the heavy shadows at the front wall and stepped into the sunlight. They saw her in silhouette. Judging from the height of the door, Fargo estimated the shapely female would be about five feet, eight inches tall. Her hair fell below her broad shoulders. She presented a small waist that flowed nicely to form the beginning of her curvy hipline. She wore a billowy long-sleeve blouse and skirt. The hem of the skirt almost touched the floor. The light at her back outlined her thighs and legs through the skirt. She stood with her slender legs parted slightly. Fargo was immediately aroused.

They watched her pass through the shaft of strong light and come down the aisle to them. She looked at Father Bonelli but spoke to Fargo. "You would be an idiot to go after a dozen armed men. They will kill you." Looking at Fargo, she added, "You have seen the coffins outside?"

The stately woman's oval face captivated Fargo. She had a Cupid's-bow mouth; full lower lip and perfectly symmetrical peaks on the upper lip, the corners turned up slightly, giving her a pleasant appearance. Her eyelashes were long, black, and curled. The dark-brown eyebrows arched in a line directly above the soft-brown pupils of her almond-shaped eyes, then angled down beautifully. She also had a perfect nose, upturned and with a narrow bridge. He glanced at her honey-brown hair, noticed the widow's peak of her hairline and that she wore no rings.

Fargo touched the brim of his hat. "Yes, ma'am. I saw them. You've seen that long row of dead Indians out there in the sun?"

"Yes. I watched you shoot them."

Father Bonelli asked, "And your name is . . . ?"

Her gaze stayed on Fargo's lake-blue eyes. "Marie Mercier."

Fargo began to frown. "Felix Mercier's, er—"

"Niece," she replied quickly. "Uncle Felix was murdered during the night. We were on a wagon—"

"I found the bodies," Fargo interrupted. "How did you manage to escape? Seemed to me whoever massacred them knew what they were doing."

"I don't know how they got in without being noticed. It happened ever so fast. One second everyone was asleep, so silent, so peaceful. The next second, guns fired throughout the circled wagons. A man shot Uncle Felix in the head. I sat up and he shot at me but missed. I fell back as though the bullet had struck me. The man left. After he did, I put a finger to the blood on my uncle's forehead and smeared it on mine so they would see it if anyone came back to check.

"I lay still and listened to them talk, arguing about what to do next. Some wanted to stay until dawn, others insisted they stick to their plan and leave immediately. Those wanting to go won the argument.

"Before they rode off, they came back inside the wagons and stole our money and valuables. I held my breath while a foul-smelling man removed my jewelry. He took the silver necklace and bracelet my grandmother gave me on my eighteenth birthday. I've worn that necklace every day for the last twelve years."

Marie shifted her gaze to Padre Bonelli's drawn face. "Like your priceless figurine, my family heirlooms are now gone, lost forever." As she spoke, her hand dipped into the wide left pocket of her skirt. She brought out the silver compact and opened it. Inspecting her lips reflected in the mirror on the inside of the lid, she sighed, "Gone forever."

"Maybe not," Fargo suggested. "I don't care how fast they ride or where. I'll find them and bring back your jewelry, and the statuette."

"Sir, those are twelve desperate men," she told him emphatically. "Alone, you won't stand a chance. Yes, the loss of my heirlooms is tragic, but believe me, they're not worth you committing suicide in an attempt to retrieve them. I beg you not to go on my behalf."

Bonelli seemed touched by her sincerity. Glancing at the empty niche, Bonelli sighed, then said, "The lady is correct, Mr. Fargo. In view of what she has told us about these murderers, I now believe you should not pursue them. Perhaps God felt we no longer needed Our Lady."

Fargo thought briefly. Something bothered him, something she had said, but he couldn't put his finger on it. Finally he commented, "No. I'll catch up to them. When I do, they will die quickly. Both of you will get your priceless items back."

When he turned to leave, Marie grabbed his shirt sleeve and stopped him. Looking up into his eyes, she said, "Sir, if you insist on going after them, then I'll ride with you."

"No," Fargo replied curtly. "The desert's no place for a female, certainly not one as lovely as you." Again he touched the brim of his hat.

Marie insisted, "Mr. Fargo, please let me come with you. You need me there. I can recognize at least two of the men on sight, and I know most all of their voices."

"Won't be necessary, ma'am, but thanks anyway. Simple truth is, when the first shot is fired, I don't want to look after anybody else's hide but my own. You'd only be in the way. You'd probably get both of us killed."

They watched him turn and head for the door, then they followed and stood in the doorway. The priest made one last plea. "There are only four horses in Domingo. I can get four of the men to ride with you."

As Fargo whistled loudly for the Ovaro, he shook his head. Waiting for the pinto, he looked over his shoulder and said, "Padre, they'd be more in the way than Miss Mercier. Thanks just the same. However, you can tell me one thing."

Bonelli stepped out onto the landing. "Yes?"

"Where do you think they might be going? What's out there?"

"Nothing that I know of," he answered. "I have never been that way."

Fargo looked at Marie and repeated his questions. She shook her head. "Don't go," she implored.

The Ovaro trotted across the square to Fargo. He climbed up in the saddle and looked at the priest and woman, saying, "In my hip pocket is a letter from Felix Mercier. Next to it is the money he paid me. He hired me to take him to Guaymos on the west coast of Mexico. Now, lady, since you were traveling with him, you're going to tell me why you didn't mention the letter."

Marie came down several steps, shaking her head. She stopped and replied, "This is news to me, Mr. Fargo. My uncle never mentioned your name or that our destination was Guaymos. I find it odd he kept this secret from me. I always understood our destination was Baja California. That is all we talked about back in New Orleans. You are positive you aren't mistaken?"

"The letter says Guaymos. That is southwest of here, isn't it?"

"I wouldn't know," she answered.

Bonelli shrugged.

Fargo turned the Ovaro and headed for the south gate without saying another word or looking back. He stopped outside the cantina and called for Lupita to bring him a bottle of whiskey.

"*Sí, señor,*" he heard her shout, her voice laced with happiness. Seconds later she came through the doorway, clutching two amber bottles to her bosom.

Taking them, he said, "You be here when I return and we'll finish what Padre Bonelli so rudely interrupted. *Está bien,* niña?"

"*Sí.* Where are you going? When will you come back?"

Chachona stepped into the doorway as he told Lupita, "I'm going to get the statue. Look for me in two or three days."

"Don't go," Chachona warned.

Fargo chuckled. "Seems like everybody is telling me that." He leaned down and kissed Lupita on the mouth, then nudged the Ovaro forward.

At the stable, he made the stallion ready for hard riding, then urged him to drink and dipped water from the bucket for himself. Within minutes he rode through the south opening in the protective adobe wall and began a switchback to spot the murdering thieves' trail. On the return leg, he found ten sets of shod hoofprints and one unshod set. He wheeled the pinto around and followed the trail.

He rode at a walk all day under the blistering hot sun, but he had no trouble staying on the desperadoes' tracks, clearly visible in the hot sand.

Dust devils sprang up all around him and pirouetted

across the desert to become lost from sight in the rippling waves of heat.

Occasionally Fargo would halt to rest the stallion and wet the pinto's tongue and his own with a few drops of his precious water, then he would remount and press onward.

In midafternoon four buzzards had appeared overhead, circled twice, then flew southwest. Fargo didn't like them watching him.

As the sun lowered and bumped the horizon, he watched a fat gila monster emerge from under a spate of flat rocks and look around for a handy meal.

Soon a diamondback, longer than his leg, bigger around than his forearm, with its long wide beads of rattles marking the sand, slithered across the Ovaro's path. Fargo didn't care for the deadly snake either.

Moments later he looked ahead and saw several buzzards on the ground. They watched him approach until the pinto was practically on them, then they hopped away a distance. He reined the horse to a halt and looked down on the sun-parched water hole. Six skeletal remains surrounded the hole. He noticed all of their clothing and weapons were missing.

He dismounted to rest the pinto and stretch the kinks from his body. He turned and looked into the sun, now halfway down the horizon and fiery red-orange as ever, and saw the silhouettes of four horsemen riding toward the dry water hole.

His right hand hung only inches away from the handle of his holstered big Colt as he stood watching them ride up and halt. All were Mexicans, and they were all bearded, mustachioed, and soaked with sweat. They were armed with French-made pistols and rifles. Snaggle-toothed bandoliers crisscrossed their chests. Three were rather short and ratty-looking. The other was taller, paunchy, and looked downright mean.

"*Bandidos*," Fargo muttered.

Breaking a gap-toothed smile, the larger man dropped to the ground and said in a garrulous voice, *"Buenos días, señor."* Shifting to English, he added, "The hole, it has no water?"

Fargo watched the man's companions dismount and separate. "Looks that way," he replied.

"Where are you going, *amigo*?" the man asked. He waved a hand before him. "There's nothing here."

The other three men drifted to positions that spread them around him in a semicircle.

Fargo replied easily, softly, with sincerity in his tone, "You're here. I'm looking for twelve real bad men. Texicans. Butchers and thieves. Seen them?"

"Oh, no, *señor*," the bull of a man quickly answered, "there are no such men out here." He cut his eyes among the other three evil faces and asked in Spanish, "Did you see twelve bad men today?"

They grunted no.

The fellow shrugged, splayed his hands, and said, "They haven't seen any men today, *señor*. That's a nice horse you ride. Maybe you want to give it to me, *sí*?"

"Not in this life," Fargo answered.

As the big fellow stepped toward the Ovaro, two of his companions moved closer to Fargo while drawing their guns. Fargo drew the Colt, fired twice, and shot the two men on his right. Their leader stopped in midstride and looked at them sprawled on the ground. "Aw, *amigo*, why did you shoot my friends like that. I wanted to pat your big horse, that's all. Now you've made me very mad."

Fargo aimed between the man's eyes but spoke to the other *bandido* in Spanish. "Drop that rifle and mount up. Make one false move and both of you will be left here for buzzard meat."

The little man obeyed, but when he was on his horse, Fargo saw his hand reach for the pistol stuck in his waistband. The Colt barked once. The slow-handed man catapulted over his horse's rump. The Colt instantly moved back to the sole survivor. Fargo hissed, "I'm letting you live so you can go back to wherever you came from and spread the word that one mean Anglo is on the loose here in this part of Mexico. *Comprende*?"

"Oh, *Sí, señor, sí, sí*, but El Jefe, he's not going to like you shooting these men."

Fargo believed the fear he saw in the man's widened eyes was genuine. "Then mount up and get the hell out of my sight *muy ligero*."

"*Sí, señor*, I go now. No problem, *señor*."

Fargo watched him get in the saddle, turn his horse, and trot off in a westerly direction. After the man rode out of range, Fargo mounted and returned to the desperadoes' trail.

Shortly before midnight, the moon rose and made things easier for the Trailsman. An hour later, he found where the Texicans had stopped and made a small cooking fire with clumps of desert grass, long since dried brittle by the sun. He decided to rest for the night, thinking he'd catch up with them later the next day. He unsaddled the stallion, spread his bedroll, undressed, and stretched out on it. He gazed at the stars, then drifted to sleep.

Fargo's wild-creature hearing snapped his eyes open. He stayed on his side, listening. A horse was approaching at a walk from the northeast. Rolling onto his back, he moved the Colt to his groin. Raising his head slightly, he looked down his body. His feet framed a moon-bathed rider and horse coming straight toward the bedroll.

Fargo's eyes focused an inch below the brim of the rider's *sombrero*. Slowly the Colt lifted. He began applying pressure on the trigger, paused, and held when the rider halted about twenty yards away and eased off the saddle. The stranger stayed beside the horse's head as both walked toward him.

Fargo dipped the Colt's barrel and squeezed the trigger.

The horse snorted, reared, and jerked the intruder up and back. Pulling on the reins, the rider held back the horse. "Whoa, Lady Ruth, whoa," the woman from New Orleans cried. "Easy, girl. Why did you do that, Mr. Fargo? You could have gotten me killed."

"Honey, I saved your life. Look on the other side of your horse, there on the ground in front of her."

A rattler at least six feet long lay stretched full-length on the sand.

"I thought it was a dead tree limb," she gasped.

"Tree limb?" he snorted. "What tree?"

She patted the mare's neck, dropped the reins, and came to him.

He propped on an elbow, looked up at her face, and said, "I thought I told you—"

She spun her back to him, cutting him off. "I know what you said."

"Ma'am, don't ever sneak up on a sleeping man like that again. It's a fast way to get killed."

She glanced over her shoulder at him. "Oh? How do you propose I approach a sleeping man?"

He sat up. "From upwind."

She half-turned. "Upwind?"

"That way he can smell you coming."

Her body stiffened. She looked around. Finally, she smiled and asked, "Will you allow me to ride with you, or must I follow at a discreet distance?"

"Suit yourself," he replied, and reclined.

He watched her go to the mare and get her bedroll. She spread it out on the ground a good fifteen feet to the left of his.

As though he couldn't see, she started undressing. First she removed the hat and the small yellow bow that held back her hair. Hooking her thumbs in the waist of her long underdrawers, she worked them off. Then she removed the billowy blouse. Fargo watched twin voluptuous breasts pop free. They hung low and swung sensually when she withdrew her arms from the sleeves. As she knelt and slipped inside the bedroll, he marveled at her shapely rump accentuated briefly in the moonglow.

Fargo put his back to her and went to sleep.

4

Fargo awakened at dawn to see Marie Mercier dressed, sitting on her bedroll and watching him from over the lid of her compact. Through a winsome smile she asked, "Was I up or downwind?"

"Down," he suggested. "Had to be, or else I wouldn't have gotten a wink of sleep."

"Do we have any coffee?"

"If we do, will you know how to brew it?"

"Of course. Why would you ask that?"

"A hunch, a feeling. Those soft hands don't look as though they've ever done a day's work. You don't look like the kitchen type."

"You're correct, Mr. Fargo, on both counts. But—"

"No but to it, ma'am," he interjected. "I don't have coffee to waste with somebody who's never fixed any. You scrounge up an armful of dry grass while I pull on my clothes. I'll brew the coffee."

He watched her rise, then look at him a second or two before walking away. By the time he had dressed and was pulling on his boots, she came back with the grass. He got his small pot ready to brew, then made a fire and set the pot on its edge. While waiting for it to boil, they chatted.

"I understood you're from New Orleans."

"Yes," she answered, "but not originally. We have a cotton plantation in Mississippi. I was born and reared there. I left at age sixteen to attend Mrs. Alice Priddy's

42

Finishing School for Young Ladies in Boston. Hated every minute of it."

Fargo suspected she had a dark story to tell. "But you stayed, of course, whether you wanted to or not."

"Certainly. What else could I do? I came home during the summers—the first two, that is. I was confused, mixed up. In Boston, all I thought about was going home to Mississippi, back to Firestone Plantation. Then, after I got there, all I thought about was returning to Boston."

"So, how'd it end?"

"It didn't. I simply grew up, matured. After Mrs. Priddy's, two of the other young women and I took a place in Boston for two years."

"Are you saying you went to work? Actually worked?"

"On, no. Money was the least of our worries."

"Then you played."

Her eyes kicked up sharply. "The coffee's boiling."

He filled two tin cups, saying, "After you got tired of playing, you went back to Mississippi."

"Yes. Actually, Uncle Felix came and got me."

"The two of you were close?"

"Very."

When Marie didn't volunteer more, he changed the subject. "Do you have a gun?"

"No. I'm afraid of firearms."

He shook his head, downed the last of his coffee, then stood. "What in the hell are you doing wandering around Mexico without any means of protecting yourself? Woman, this is hostile territory. You're the one who warned me not to go, and I've got two weapons."

She dumped the rest of her coffee on the sand and stood. "I'm not totally defenseless, Mr. Fargo. I do have a—"

His raised hand stopped her. Grinning, he said, "Lady, your body won't defend you. It could get you in more trouble than you might imagine."

"I was about to say I do have a bullwhip."

"Bullwhip?"

"Yes. And I do know how to use it. Whipping is one of the first things I learned how to do on Firestone. My father was a good teacher."

Fargo glanced to her roan mare and saw the coiled bullwhip hanging on the saddle horn. "How long is it?" he asked.

"Twenty-five feet. If need be, I can pluck out an eyeball with it."

Fargo gulped. Glancing to the eastern horizon, he said, "Let's go. With an ounce of luck, we'll catch up to them before sundown."

He packed his utensils in the saddlebags. They rolled up and secured their bedrolls in place, mounted, and rode southwest in the robbers' tracks. Less than a hundred yards from their camp site, the group's trail divided. Six turned southeast and five angled off more west than south. This puzzled Fargo.

Why, he wondered, would they split up? He stared along the tracks leading west-southwest. "Santa Ana?" he wondered aloud. Glancing at Marie, he added, "This doesn't make any sense."

She studied the other trail a moment. "Do you suppose they quarreled?"

"No, there's no sign of an argument. Look at how they parted. It's even. They knew before arriving here that they would break into two groups. The question is, which bunch has the mission's statue?"

"And my jewelry," she hastened to remind.

"Correct," he agreed.

Marie dismounted and led her mare a distance alongside the hoofprints heading southeast. She stopped, pointed down at the ground, and called out, "Over here, Mr. Fargo. I may have found the answer."

He rode to her and looked down. A silver charm bracelet lay on the sand. She stooped and picked it up.

"It's mine," she said, and slipped it around her right wrist.

"You're a lucky woman, Miss Mercier. Thousands of miles of raw desert and one scrawny bracelet on it somewhere. Not unlike the needle in a haystack. But the find doesn't necessarily mean this bunch has the statue also. One group could have taken your jewelry and the other Father Bonelli's figurine."

Again she pointed to the hoofprints. "I don't think so. One of them rides an unshod horse."

Fargo looked at her blankly. Women, he thought, have the oddest rationales. He asked anyhow. "So, what's the unshod horse got to do with it?"

A quick smile preceded her reply. "The leader of the gang rides an unshod horse."

"Oh? And how do you know this?"

"I told you I listened to them talk after they killed everybody on the wagon train. A man they called Mad Jack gave most of the orders. When I heard them getting on their horses, I peeked through a rip in the canvas cover to watch them depart. I saw one of the horses hadn't been shod. This fellow, Jack, was in the saddle. I know he was because one of the others mentioned his name twice during conversation as they rode away."

"Uh, huh. Why didn't you mention this back in Domingo?"

"I don't know. Does it matter?"

Women, Fargo thought. "No, it's unimportant now. Get back on the mare. We'll follow Mad Jack's trail. One way's as good as the other. The worst we can do is get back your necklace." He suspected that was her idea in the first place.

To Fargo's surprise the trail led to a spring-fed lagoon partly surrounded with rocks and boulders polished smooth by countless sandstorms. Watering her horse, Marie said, "Mr. Fargo, I need a bath."

He looked at her, knowing that if she stripped in front of him again, it would be midnight before they quit. He made a painful decision. "We don't have time to stop."

She took out all of the hurt when she pitched her *sombrero* on a boulder and reached to untie the bow. "Won't take but a moment," she purred. Undoing the top button on her blouse, she added, "You may sit on the shady side of the stone while I bathe."

He glanced at the boulder and saw what shade there was would deny him a view. "By all means, ma'am." Fargo moved to the shadowy ribbon and sat with his back against the warm stone, his gaze fixed on a yucca nearby. After a moment, he heard her enter the water.

"This is wonderful," she sighed. "So cool. So refreshing. Can you hear me, Mr. Fargo?"

"Yeah, I can hear," he grunted. "Make it snappy. Trail's getting cold."

"No, it isn't. They probably stopped for baths, too."

Filth avoids water, he thought, then hurried her up, saying, "Get a move on."

"Don't rush me, Mr. Fargo. I'll be out in a moment, then you can bathe."

Listening to her splash around, giggle, and coo occasionally soothed his earlier desire to hurry after the murderers. He caught himself brushing sand off his neck and wrists. He stood, keeping his back to her, and began pulling off his clothes.

"Sir, what are you doing?" she cried.

He heard her swim to the bank and leave the water. "I don't bathe in my clothes," he muttered.

While leaning against the boulder to pull off his boots, he heard her drag her garments from the top of it. "One minute and I'll be dressed," she told him.

"One minute and I'll be in that water," he mumbled.

Not caring if she saw his nakedness, he stepped around the big rock, found she was indeed a fast dresser, ran, and leapt into the pool. She turned and looked when he yelped, "You said it was cool. Dammit, woman, this water is ice-cold!"

Chuckling, she scaled the boulder and sat cross-legged to watch him. She brought the compact from the skirt pocket and opened it, asking, "Do you mind an onlooker when you bathe?"

"Not if the onlooker doesn't. You get some kind of a thrill watching men in water?"

She smiled. "No, not really. Men bathe differently than women. That's all. Seen one, seen them all. Do you prefer I not watch?" She looked in the mirror and inspected one eye then the other.

"Lady, I don't give a damn what you do." He surface-dived, swam underwater a short distance, then stood in knee-deep water.

Marie's eyes widened and her left hand flew to her mouth to catch the gasp that escaped from it. "Oh, my," she gulped quite unladylike. "I know you are a big man, but I never dreamed—"

"What did you say?" he asked. "Speak up."

"I said it's getting late in the day."

Walking onto the bank, he watched her averted eyes flick back to him, and as they did, she blushed. At the boulder, he looked up at her and said, "Seen one, seen them all." He winked, then moved around the stone to his clothes. Pulling them on, he decided to test her spunk. "How do you feel about being my decoy?"

Frowning slightly, she snapped the lid closed and turned to face him. "I don't understand."

"When we see them, I'll break away and ride a fast circle to get in position ahead of them. You stop and give me time, then shuck your clothes and ride straight for them. They will be so preoccupied watching you that they won't see me. Two shakes of a long slender leg and we'll have them. Decoy."

"Mr. Fargo, I think that is a bad idea. No, I couldn't do such a thing. There must be another way."

"Okay, what's your suggestion."

"The same as they did to us back at the wagon train."

That was his exact plan. The woman has an evil mind, he decided, and a damned fast one to boot. He smiled up at her. "Good idea, ma'am. I'll shoot ten while you whip one to death."

Now she smiled wickedly, shot him a wink, and replied, "Mr. Fargo, you underestimate me. I'll have five beat to death before you fire the first shot." She slipped off the boulder and strode to the mare, as though there was no doubt in her mind.

Fargo grinned all the way to the pinto. She's got guts, he thought. Mounting up, he added, "Mean as a rattler."

"What was that?" she asked. "A rattler? Where?"

"Nothing, ma'am, just mumbling to myself." He spurred the Ovaro to walk.

They rode with their backs to the sun till it set. The hoofprints were clear enough for tracking at night. He wanted to press on, but she didn't. "Please, Mr. Fargo, can we stop and rest for the night? I'm terribly tired. You were right. I should not have come. I'm sorry."

Fargo thought a moment. He believed he was close to the gang. He wanted to spot their camp and be in position to strike when they were asleep. He considered leaving her behind, but then changed his mind when the big Mexican bandido flashed to mind. There was no way of knowing what would happen if he found her. Fargo looked into Marie's tired eyes and nodded.

Sighing heavily, obviously quite relieved, she slid from the saddle.

Doing likewise, Fargo commented, "We sleep until midnight, then it's back in the saddle."

Removing her bedroll from behind her saddle, she queried, "Fine with me, sir. Only, how do we know when it's midnight? Neither of us has a timepiece."

He chuckled. "I've got a timepiece in my brain. I'll set it to awaken me."

Spreading out her bedroll, she frowned and asked, "Yes, but how will you know it's midnight? I don't even know what time it is right now."

Again Fargo chuckled. "It's about seven o'clock. The Big Dipper will tell us when it's midnight."

She looked skyward. "How?"

"You're looking in the wrong place." He pointed to a bright star. "That's the North Star. When the Big Dipper is directly to the left of it, the hour is midnight. Never fails." He dropped his bedroll next to hers.

"Amazing," she muttered, and worked her long legs down inside her bedroll.

As usual, Fargo stripped down to his shorts before lying on top of his bedroll. He looked up and watched the brighter stars appear first as night fell.

"Romantic, isn't it?" she whispered. "A star-filled night sky, the wide open spaces, no sounds to speak of, a big strong man, and little weak me. What are you thinking, Mr. Fargo?"

"Nothing. I'm setting the alarm on my timepiece."

"My presence doesn't disturb you? My vulnerability doesn't arouse you? Am I that undesirable? Are you afraid of females, Mr. Fargo?"

His head turned to her. "Me? Afraid of women?" He chuckled. "Hardly, Miss Mercier. You've made it plain you don't want to be bothered. I don't waste my time fawning over women who wouldn't respond favorably."

"Oh? Are you saying I'm a cold bitch?"

"No. I'm saying this isn't the time or place to determine your lineage or take your temperature. We need to close our eyes and go to sleep, not wrestle and get so exhausted we couldn't commit mass murder. And that, ma'am, is exactly why we're here. Now, tomorrow night I'll be more than happy to continue this conversation and see where it leads."

"Is that a promise?"

"Depends solely on your attitude and stamina. Good night, Miss Mercier."

As she flopped facedown, he heard her mumble an obscenity. Fargo closed his eyes and thought of the Rocky Mountains and forests while drifting to sleep.

A cool west wind awakened him. He glanced at the Big Dipper, noted the hour was ten o'clock and the leading edge of low-hanging clouds would soon pass overhead. He got under the covers and willed himself back to sleep.

Howling wind snapped his eyes open. Wind-driven sand blasted across his bedroll. He glanced toward Marie's bedroll, saw her snuggled deep inside it, then looked up, hoping to see the Big Dipper. The night sky was blotted out by the furious sandstorm. He knew that by now all signs of the band's tracks had long since disappeared. Fargo decided it was best to follow the wind and go find the men. He reached over and shook Marie's hip to awaken her.

She grunted.

A hard masculine voice growled, "Mister, you better be damn sure you show me naked hands when you bring them out from that bedroll."

5

Fargo glanced above his bedroll. Six pistols were aimed at his head. The men holding them looked as though they wouldn't mind if he chose to make a fight. All but one were standing. The other man, a large fellow with a thick black beard and a mustache that hid most of his mouth, was squatting near the head of the bedroll.

The man said, "Get on your feet, mister. While you're at it, why are you following us?"

Fargo opened the bedroll and sat up. "What makes you think I'm following you?"

The man motioned for one of his men to check the bedroll, then nodded to one of the others. The first man found the Colt. After they backed away with the weapon, the unshaven fellow said, "Don't try to bull-shit me. I know when I'm being followed and when I ain't. Get up and put your clothes on."

Fargo brought his clothes up with him when he stood. While he pulled on his shirt, the bearded man shook Marie awake. Her head poked out from her bedroll. She began an angry complaint, "Mr. Fargo, get your—" but clipped it short when she saw the men.

"Not me, ma'am." Fargo chuckled. "These desert sandstorms bring all sorts of beasts in the wind. I think they want you to get up and dress." He glanced at their chief adversary. "Right, *amigo*?"

The man nodded. Standing, he said, "Yeah, that's right."

"I don't have any undergarments on," she quipped. "Please turn your backs."

The man guffawed. "Hellfire, lady, you ain't got nothing we ain't seen before. We ain't turning our backs, so get outta there and do what I told you."

They appeared unconcerned that she might come out shooting. Fargo said, "Better watch out, mister. She's armed to the teeth." No one so much as flinched a muscle or batted an eye. Fargo pulled on his Levi's.

Marie drew her garments inside her bedroll to dress. Seconds later the top cover flew back and she reached for her riding boots. Putting them on, she looked at the large man and asked, "What's going on?"

He raked the sand-filled air with his gun hand and replied, "Aw, lady, it being such a nice night and all, I thought we'd take a night ride. Kinda thought we'd go see what's west of here. That meet with your approval, ma'am? We could leave you behind. Have to take your horse, though. Which way you want it?"

"I'm not staying out here alone," she answered crisply.

Fargo slipped into his coat, then snugged his hat down. Marie stood.

The man spoke to Fargo. "We already got your Sharps, so there's no need for you to hope we missed it." To Marie, he added, "That bullwhip's not on your saddle horn anymore either. Now, gents, here's how we're gonna travel. Big man, you ride up front with me where we can keep an eye on you. The lady rides next-to-last in the column. Just like good little pony soldiers, we're gonna ride single-file." Striding to his mount, he barked, "Alvin, you and Hawk Nose tie their hands behind them. Get a move on."

Within the minute they were bound at the wrists and put on their horses. Fargo fell in behind the bearded leader. Contrary to what Marie had told him earlier, he saw the man's horse was shod. They rode straight into the howling sandstorm.

Shortly after dawn the wind abated. The sun, hot as ever, hung as a diffused white orb in the sandy sky. By noon, it was as though the sandstorm had never occurred. Heat waves rippled above the desert floor. Fargo wondered where in the hell they were being taken, and why.

Day gave way to night, and night passed into daylight. They stopped only briefly to sleep. The men kept Marie out of Fargo's sight during the rest stop. Back in the saddle, he turned to see how she was doing. The leader ordered, "Keep your eyes forward. She's all right."

Fargo asked, "What's your name, mister?"

"McCord. Jack McCord. Some call me Mad Jack McCord."

"Why's that?"

"I get angry real easy. Then I hurt people."

"Where in hell are we going?"

Mad Jack sighed, shook his head, then said, "Don't ask so many questions. Questions make me mad."

"One more and I'll be quiet. When will we get there?"

Mad Jack McCord backhanded him across the mouth, then spurred his big dun stallion ahead.

Fargo ran his tongue over and inside his lips, found no traces of blood, and thought, McCord, you don't know it, but now *I'm* angry.

The day passed slowly. Finally, the scorching sun lowered below the horizon. Mad Jack kept going. Fargo watched the Big Dipper move downward slowly from above and to the left of the North Star. The faithful timepiece indicated the hour was ten o'clock when McCord halted the column and told everyone to catch a few winks of sleep.

Again, they separated their captives, and Fargo wondered why. If they were molesting her, she was taking it while biting her tongue, for he never once heard her whimper or voice a complaint.

Mad Jack had them back in their saddles by four o'clock. Dawn broke. Fargo's lake-blue eyes were focused on McCord's back. Again, the Trailsman tested the security of his wrist bindings and found them tight. All he wanted was one chance, one moment alone with McCord. The mere thought of choking the man to death caused his big hands to double into fists.

At midmorning, Fargo glanced toward the southwestern horizon. A fuzzy black line of horsemen bobbed in the shimmering waves of heat. He said nothing. A few moments later one of the men behind him whined, "Hey, McCord! We got company. Up ahead. Off to your right. Whaddaya make out of it?"

Mad Jack's head angled right slightly. "I see 'em," he shouted back. "Nothing to get worried about. We can handle 'em easy enough."

Within minutes it was obvious the two groups were on a course to intercept one another. As they closed in, Fargo counted ten horsemen, all wearing big *sombreros*. This should prove interesting, he mused to himself. The horsemen came just out of gun range, changed course, and rode parallel to Mad Jack's column.

Damn good maneuver, Fargo thought. Nothing is more unnerving than playing a game of Mexican sweat to intimidate the other fellow. He decided to help the Texicans by aggravating McCord. "Mad Jack, it sure does look like we're outnumbered two to one."

"Shut your mouth, Fargo."

"Untie my hands and give me my Colt. I'll go chase them off for you cowards."

McCord dropped back and swung a fist at Fargo's head, but Fargo dodged away and the blow grazed his jaw. "I told you to keep quiet," Mad Jack growled.

54

"Next time I'll pull you to the ground and beat you."

"Uh, huh," Fargo replied, and let it go at that.

McCord resumed his position at the head of the column. Fargo wondered what the man was thinking. He wondered what the men in the other group were thinking.

The two bands continued to ride parallel. The sun reached its zenith and began descending. Occasionally Fargo heard McCord muttering to himself.

The blazing hot sun lowered and touched the horizon without any closure by either group. Fargo wondered if the others were actually waiting for night before they attacked. Surely not, he considered inwardly. In the dark they wouldn't be able to tell friend from foe.

The situation soon clarified itself and foretold their intentions. Fargo watched them shift into a gallop and ride into the setting sun. So that's it, he thought. They want their backs to the sun when they attack. Good move.

The same whining voice spoke from behind Fargo. This time there was a pronounced edge of concern in the tone. "Whatcha want us to do, McCord? They're gonna jump us for sure."

Mad Jack proceeded straight ahead, as though he hadn't heard the warning nor seen the threat forming ahead of him.

The Mexicans rode hard for a depression that cut across the flat terrain from horizon to horizon as it meandered north to south. A tinge of excitement from the column of thirsty horses predicted water flowed or stood in the depression.

All eyes in the column watched the Mexicans enter the low spot and nearly disappear before emerging. On the far side they formed in a line to face and wait for the Texicans. Fargo imagined himself viewing the scene from above. He saw it as a T with the stream in front of the newcomers. The stream became a water barrier Mad Jack and his men must cross.

The fiery red-rimmed silhouette of a Mexican stood out from all the others. The giant of a man was centered in the line of horsemen. Fargo reckoned he gave the orders.

Confrontation was imminent if it was to occur during the last rays of daylight. Both groups seemed determined to stand their ground, with the Mexicans as the immovable object and the outnumbered Texicans as the irresistible force. Mad Jack maintained the column's walking speed and stayed on the collision course.

About thirty yards shy of the low spot, McCord raised a hand and halted his men.

Fargo wanted loose. He needled McCord. "I know this is going to piss you off, but your cry-baby back there asked a damn good question. There's a heap of difference between being mad and insane. Those bastards have you outnumbered and outgunned. Don't be an idiot, McCord. You need every gun you can bring to bear. Tell one of your men to untie me. Hell, I'll help you shoot them, if for no other reason than to save my own hide. What do you say?"

"Shut your goddamn mouth, Fargo. I ain't letting you go." Over the shoulder he shouted, "All right, you men, move up and get in a line. We're gonna charge the bastards." He looked at Fargo, grinned, and winked. "You can stay put or ride for Sunday. Makes no difference to me. After it's over, I'll chase you down and bring you back."

Watching the Texicans form up, Fargo decided he'd stay and see how the fight would come out. Most of all he wanted himself and his thirsty Ovaro down in that water.

He looked down the line to find Marie and saw her at the far end. Her hands were not tied. Odd, he thought.

In that instant, Mad Jack McCord, let out a loud whoop and charged. The entire line followed him over the rough terrain. Everybody yelled, beat their mounts to go faster, and leaned forward to make the smallest possible target. The Mexicans drew their pistols and rushed to engage them in the stream. Halfway to the stream both groups started firing.

Fargo trotted along behind the Texicans to observe the melee and learn the depth of the water before taking the pinto into it. Neither force lost a man during the first exchange of gunfire, of which there was plenty. Fargo blamed the Texicans' poor marksmanship on the uneven ground, which made their gun hands unsteady, and the fact that they were looking into the sun. He figured the Mexicans missed because of the same ground problem and because their weapons were inferior.

Both groups clashed in the middle of the wide stream. Within seconds the riders became entwined and turned their mounts, shot wildly, shoved, and otherwise tried to dislodge their foes from their saddles. To Fargo it was more a show of horsemanship than gunmanship, and it was hard to tell who was better at it.

Fargo saw the water was shallow. He nudged the Ovaro to enter it upstream about fifteen yards from the battle. He slid from the saddle and sat chest-deep in the cool water to drink and watch the fracas. He noted the Mexicans were more interested in Marie than they were in the Texicans. It was as though they wanted to take her alive.

Four men surrounded her mare. One leapt from his saddle with arms outstretched to grab Marie and take her into the water with him. She shot him in midair, then swung and shot another off his mount.

Where did Marie get a gun? Fargo wondered.

McCord knocked a man out of the saddle, wheeled, and shot him dead where the fellow knelt in the water.

Fargo saw a fourth Mexican splash, dead. Through the gunfire he heard men scream but couldn't tell if it was from being wounded or if they were simply screaming for the hell of it.

The virtual hand-to-hand combat had been going on for quite awhile, and Fargo sensed they were tiring and trying to disengage. As suddenly as they had clashed, they parted and rode up opposite banks. Fargo heard the Mexican leader shout "*Vámonos*!" to his men, and their mounts' hooves pound away.

Mad Jack sent two of his men to bring Fargo to him. "Nice of you to stay and watch," McCord said dryly. "Saved me wasting time to chase you down." He shouted for everybody to get back in a column. They followed the stream for about a mile before crossing it. McCord led the column toward the thin arc of the setting sun.

Fargo glanced over his shoulder and saw Marie in her position at the rear. Her wrists were still not bound. Why isn't she here, up front, where she belongs? he thought. Not only does she lie, the bitch is damn cool in battle and handles a pistol like a man, a mean man.

Fargo wondered about many other things as darkness fell. McCord kept the column moving relentlessly onward. He didn't halt until shortly after midnight, and then only for two hours.

Lying on the sand, Fargo asked him, "What's the big hurry, McCord?" He wanted to ask questions about Marie, about why she had been armed earlier, then allowed to ride unbound. But he held those questions in check, deciding that they would be answered in time.

"You're doing it again, Fargo," McCord quipped.

"Making you angry?"

"That's right. Just shut up and go to sleep. You'll learn soon enough."

Fargo closed his eyes. The big ugly bastard had told

him what he wanted to hear: the trip was about to end.

Mad Jack McCord roused everybody at about two in the morning. Hawk Nose stood next to the Ovaro to help Fargo mount. The young man had a bloody neckerchief tied around his forehead. "Ain't nothing," he told Fargo.

The big man really didn't need any help, but he wanted to question Hawk Nose, so he let his foot slip from the stirrup. Hawk Nose grabbed to brace him up. For a moment their faces were only a few inches apart.

Fargo said, "Thanks, fella. I must still be half-asleep. Where in the hell are we, anyhow? You know where we're going?"

Hawk Nose seemed leery to answer. He stammered, "er," a few times and Fargo noticed he cut his eyes to McCord each time. Fargo saw that McCord was out of earshot and busy cinching up his saddle.

"C'mon, kid, tell me something. He can't hear."

"Mister, I don't know where we are. None of us do. Don't know where we're going, neither. Mad Jack and the wo—"

Too late, Hawk Nose tried to trap the reference to Marie. Fargo wedged into the breach. "She knows?"

"I already said too much. Put your boot in the stirrup and I'll boost you up."

Fargo got in the saddle without any aid from Hawk Nose. Looking down at the man, he asked, "Does she—"

Hawk Nose broke in and answered uneasily. "She's the boss. That's what you wanted to know, ain't it?"

"No," Fargo replied. "I had already figured as much. I wanted to know if she knows where that statue went."

"Beats me, mister."

Mad Jack shouted for the column to move out.

Hawk Nose went to his horse and mounted up. Fargo nudged the pinto to a walk and fell in behind McCord.

Fargo tried to remember the geographical layout here in the northern part of Mexico. Guaymos kept flashing to mind. The letter from Felix Mercier mentioned Guaymos. But the town is on the seacoast, Fargo mused, southwest of here and several day's ride. McCord said I'd learn soon enough, Fargo recalled. Several days isn't soon, so Guaymos can't be their destination. Santa Ana isn't too far from here. Could that be their destination? Is that where the other group took the statue?

He was still pondering his questions when dawn broke. With the sunlight came a dramatic change in scenery. Not only did the terrain take on a new shape, so did the flora. Splotches of grass swayed in the light breeze. While there were still yucca, there were also stands of trees. The almost-flat desert floor gave way to rises and gullies. At first, Fargo thought he saw a line of clouds low on the western horizon. After studying the hazy shapes a few minutes, he realized they were mountains.

By noon, the shapes were clearly defined. Though they weren't towering, snow-covered peaks, neither were they mere hills. The coloration told Fargo that no forests grew on them.

In the midafternoon, he watched a black hump appear between the column and the mountains. Riding closer, he saw the hump was a towering formation of black rocks with rounded peaks worn smooth by wind-driven sand. It was as though long ago a mighty upheaval shot them from the bowels of hell. He counted six huge stones.

After passing the ominous rock formation, Fargo squinted his lake-blue eyes and stared ahead at the low outline of a village. A stream—he figured it was probably the same one in which the skirmish had taken place—flowed well off to his right and toward the village. McCord moved aside, motioned for the others to proceed, then reined his mount to a halt and looked to the rear. Fargo waited a few seconds before he looked to see what Mad Jack was up to. McCord joined the rear of the column. Fargo returned his gaze to the village.

In a few moments, Mad Jack and Marie galloped past him, heading for the village.

Fargo shouted, "Where are we?"

Marie called back, "Las Rocas."

6

The adobe wall surrounding Las Rocas came into view. The village had been built on the banks of the lazy stream that cut through the center of the wall, to the left of the crumbled edges of the entrance. Fargo noticed none of the villagers was outside the adobe bulwark. This meant the Texicans had overcome any resistance and were now in control of the little town.

Approaching the entrance, Fargo heard a loud party in progress in the village. There was much laughter— male and female—whooping and hollering. Pistols fired sporadically. The drunken revelry grew louder as they rode into a narrow dusty street lined with single-level adobe structures. All the doors in the adobe hovels were closed. The people were obviously more willing to suffer unbearable heat than to expose themselves to the Anglos.

Hawk Nose and Alvin moved up to ride ahead of Fargo. As they passed him, Hawk Nose grinned and said, "Buck up, Fargo, trip's about over."

They crossed over a little bridge that spanned a narrow part of the stream and led to the northwest corner of the plaza. The east bank of the stream formed the west side of the plaza, or *zócalo* as these people called the town square. Another narrow bridge, barren of side rails, crossed the stream where it began widening and running shallow through and over rocks near the center of the western edge of the plaza. The bridge led to a strip of barren ground at the north end of a large two-story structure, where there was an outside stairway. A wide canopied balcony ran the full length of the second level. The stairway went up to the balcony. Trees grew along the east bank of the stream.

The community well stood in the middle of the zócalo. Beyond it, an old mission almost identical to the one in Domingo fronted most of the east side of the square. The main difference between the two showed in the designs of the domes on the bell towers. This one was larger. It was painted dark blue, trimmed in yellow, and supported by numerous columns instead of four walls with arched openings like the one at Domingo. Long rows of connected one-story adobe dwellings began on the north and south edges of the plaza. The rows were separated by dusty streets that were hardly more than corridors. They formed a labyrinth inside the pitiful protective wall.

Fargo saw the rope used for tolling the mission bell hung down from the bell and alongside the outer surface of the bell tower. The body of a priest dangled from the end of the rope, a hanging noose around his neck.

To the left and right of the dead priest's feet were the crumpled, twisted bodies of seven *federales*. Clearly, they'd been made to stand next to the mission wall when they were shot to death. None wore blindfolds. All had their hands tied behind their backs. Numerous peasants had also been murdered. Their twisted bodies lay in the sun, which beat down steadily on the zócalo, where the peasants had fled for safety. A large yellow dog lay dead in a puddle of its own blood near the community well.

Because none of the bodies was bloated, Fargo knew the murders had occurred less than twenty-four hours earlier, probably late in the previous afternoon.

The hub of the Texicans' drunken party occurred on the canopied balcony.

Scantily clad *señoritas* sat on several of the Texicans' laps. Some of the men wore bloody bandages. Tables covered with whiskey bottles stood within easy reach. Four peasant men strummed guitars. Their shaky voices conveyed their terror as they sang.

Following alongside the gurgling stream, Fargo watched Hawk Nose and Alvin ride over the bridge, dismount, and go up the stairs to join the party. Fargo halted the Ovaro on the far end of the bridge.

Mad Jack shoved a young naked woman off his lap and came to stand at the balcony railing. He tilted his head back and raised an amber bottle to his mouth. He wiped the back of his hand across his lips, looked down at Fargo, and said, "Now you know the answers to your questions."

"Not quite all," Fargo replied. "Where's the statue you thieves stole?"

McCord laughed. When he did, his men laughed too. Because the men laughed, so did the frightened women. McCord gulped down the remainder of the whiskey, then flung the empty bottle down in the stream. "What statue?" he asked, glancing among his men. "Any of you men seen a statue?" Heads shook and voices claimed no knowledge. McCord shrugged a helpless gesture, then ordered, "Mullins, you and J.T. there take him around back. Sawtooth will meet you and show you where to put him."

Reluctant to leave the fun, the two men rose and headed for the stairs. McCord pointed a finger at a man with a shirt sleeve rolled up and a bloodstained bandage wrapped around his upper arm. "Sawtooth, get over here."

All Fargo wanted was a trace of slack in his bindings. He tried to get it while being led to the rear of the building and again while waiting for Sawtooth to make his appearance. With great pain, he'd managed to wrench noticeable slack in the rawhide but not enough to shake free by the time Sawtooth opened a wide door and stepped outside.

"In here, gents," he told them.

As they entered, one on either side of Fargo, both with strong grips on his upper arms, Sawtooth jammed the neck of a whiskey bottle into each man's free hand.

The room was dark. It also smelled like a livery that had never been cleaned. Sawtooth struck a match and mumbled, "There's supposed to be a lantern. Anybody see it?"

During the flaring of the match, Fargo glanced about, saw that a donkey was tethered to the far wall and that the floor was earthen. He estimated its dimensions would be at least thirty by fifty feet. The heavy wood beams supporting the floor above were within easy reach. The lantern stood just inside the door.

Sawtooth struck another match and lit it. Now Fargo saw another door in the wall to his left and presumed that's how Sawtooth got in. He wondered what was behind the door, where it led, other than to the balcony.

Sawtooth said, "Well, mister, Mad Jack said we gotta take off all your clothes. We can do it one of two ways, easy or hard. Makes me no difference. Whatcha say?"

"Hell, I know when I'm outnumbered. You won't get a fuss out of me, Sawtooth. I'd really like a slug of that whiskey, though."

The filthy man hesitated a few seconds, then nodded to J.T. He lifted his bottle to Fargo's eager lips and let him down a long swig.

When he drew the bottle away, Fargo smacked his lips and said, "Goddamn, but that was good. Sawtooth, you and these two are real friends."

He turned his back to them and stuck out his wrists so they could untie the rawhide.

J.T. set the bottle on the ground so he could use both hands to undo the bindings. Fargo felt the tension releasing. The rawhide left his wrists. His hands closed and opened a few times to increase the blood's circulation. With renewed feeling in them, he spun and swung a fist hard against Sawtooth's head.

As he cocked a left to power the fist into J.T.'s gut, shooting stars blossomed in his brain for an instant. Just as quickly they burned out, leaving a black void complete with absolute silence.

Fargo regained consciousness several hours later. It came very slowly. First he heard a buzzing. The unique mixture of aromas common to a barnyard flooded his nostrils. Finally his eyelids fluttered open. He brought the dark forms of the overhead beams into focus. Now he realized the buzzing came from the wings of a horsefly skipping across his right ear. When he tried to swat the nuisance, he found he could not move. He discovered he was flat on his back with his arms and legs spread, his hands and ankles tied to stakes. He raised his head and looked down his naked body.

They had staked him down in the middle of the room, with his head toward the door Sawtooth used. Ribbons of dust-filled light shone through several cracks in the wide door on his right. Laughter, muted by the walls and the floors above, filtered into the space. The merrymakers were going at it hard.

Fargo strained on the ropes holding him down, found them tight, definitely secure. He relaxed. Staring up at the beams, he muttered, "Okay, Fargo, try to figure out how you're going to get out of here." He concluded he had only two choices: struggle in the hope that he could pull one of the stakes out of the ground, or lay back and wait for them to make the next move and maybe commit an error in judgment that would set him free.

He opted for the first choice and started testing the four stakes. While he felt small movement in all four, he knew they were in too deep for him to dislodge. Still, he kept tugging at them, resting once in a while before trying again while listening to Marie Mercier's wild men and their women raise hell.

They were still going strong when the ribbons of light faded out. Night consumed Las Rocas, and the room became pitch-black. "At least, the damn fly's gone for the night," Fargo muttered. "Hey! Anybody out there?" he shouted. "Dammit, I'm thirsty! Hungry, too!" No voice answered. No boot stomped on the floor above. He decided he was indeed alone and forgotten. "Forgotten? Shit, maybe they intend to leave me here to die and rot." The sobering words put him back to work testing the stakes.

His body was covered with sweat and his muscles were burning from his relentless efforts to work himself free when he heard a soft sound come from somewhere above the top of his head. He lay still and listened, heard a key insert in a lock, turn, and the door grate open slowly.

"Who's there?" he called out.

The person didn't answer.

He knew somebody was standing in the doorway and reckoned Mad Jack had sent one of the men down to check on him. "Water," he said. "I need water. Go tell McCord I'm thirsty as hell and hungry enough to eat anything."

"You'll get both later," Marie's husky voice drawled.

He listened to her approach slowly and stop only inches above his head. He looked up, saw only her vague form.

"You have been wondering about many things, haven't you, Fargo?"

"A few. Mostly when you're going to feed and water your captive."

"Like I said, later. Right now you're going to listen while I talk."

"Sure, honey, but make it snappy. I'd listen much better if I had a sip of water first."

She ignored his plea and began the one-sided conversation. Sitting on the ground by his head, she said, "I will tell you how and why you came to be lashed down here.

"Your fate was sealed two days before you came across the wagon train and found everybody dead. Didn't know that, did you? Well, you had no way of knowing. That's when Uncle Felix told me about the letter he sent to you. When he made the announcement, he irrevocably signed his own death warrant.

"You see, Fargo, you were never in my plans. Or his and mine, I might add. Poor Uncle Felix. He never did know how much I hated him."

"Whoa, lady. Telling me won't clear your conscience."

She ignored his remarks and continued. "He introduced me to the bed when I was thirteen and already blossoming. It was safe because Uncle Felix couldn't make a baby. So he romped me every time he came to Firestone. And, yes, he came often.

"Two things happened. First, I began to look forward to his frequent weekend visits. Second, I couldn't stand those little boys at school. To me they were children trying to act like men. You see, after Uncle Felix came along, it took a real man to satisfy me. So, when I reached the age to marry, Daddy started inviting suitors to parties at Firestone."

"Listen, lady, I don't give a hoot about your love life. Go get me some water."

"None appealed to me," she went on, as though now talking to herself. "If they weren't sweet-smelling whiners, they were strutting fools trying to impress me with their land holdings or educations. I don't impress easily, and I cannot tolerate a whiner.

"Anyhow, Uncle Felix wasn't enough for me. I singled out Monroe, one of the plantation hands. Under threat of tearing his hide off with my whip, I had him start meeting me at a pond way back on the plantation. Monroe was about your size and had the same powerful muscles as you.

"Only Monroe was fully capable of making babies. He impregnated me. I went straight to Daddy and told him, not only about Monroe but Uncle Felix also.

"Daddy whipped Monroe to death that same night. He forbade Uncle Felix to ever again appear in his sight and promised to kill him if he ever did. Then he whisked me off to a place for unwed mothers in Boston, with instructions for the lady to dispose of the baby the instant it came from my womb."

Fargo relaxed and tried to think about the places he'd been, far away from here.

Marie continued her woeful story. "I never saw Monroe's baby. I never returned to Firestone, either. Two of the other unweds and I pooled our money and took a house in Boston. Within a month Boston's finest gentlemen were lavishing their money on us.

"The years came and went. Clara was the first to leave the nest. She took her money and went to New York City, where she married a banker. Then Louise departed with a sea captain. I stood on the dock and waved good-bye when they sailed for England. After that I worked alone.

"Then, about a year ago Uncle Felix knocked on my front door. I told him to leave, but he persisted. Between my legs, he told me about Our Lady of Guadalupe. He convinced me that it would bring enough money so neither of us would ever again have to work. What do you say to that, Fargo?"

"Get me a drink of water."

"I returned to New Orleans with him. While he was finding a buyer for his pitiful little warehouse, I worked nights in a house on Bourbon Street in the French Quarter. By day we went over our plans. We would join a wagon train taking the Santa Fe Trail to California. Uncle Felix would pay the wagon master a handsome fee to divert the wagons—under false pretense, of course—to Domingo.

"Also, he would contact a Texican he knew, have him assemble a group of men known to be handy with guns and eager to use them, and have them meet us in Domingo. Jack McCord was that man. I met and subsequently introduced him to my bed when he came to New Orleans.

"While I had him gripped between my legs, I bared my plan to him. As you know, mine was quite different from Uncle Felix's. All it took was for me to make a few additional promises for McCord to accept my plan. While I loathe him as much as I did Uncle Felix, McCord does serve a useful purpose."

"Uh, huh, I bet he does."

"Yes, well, most of them do. Brawny, rough-cut men excite me. The rougher they are, the better I like it. Where was I? Now I remember. Our delay in leaving New Orleans was because we had to find a buyer for the statue and get a firm commitment on the amount. Why purloin the damn thing if you can't get rid of it? Right, Fargo?"

He grunted.

"A wealthy man from France agreed to purchase Our Lady. Took guts for him to do that, but drooling, greedy people usually have plenty of them. Sight unseen, he paid five thousand on the spot, said fifty thousand more would be paid upon delivery to the intermediary, and four hundred forty-five thousand, the balance due, would be paid once he had it and knew for a fact it was everything Uncle Felix claimed."

70

"So, who is the intermediary?" Fargo asked, now knowing Las Rocas was not the transfer site.

"A French sea captain. His schooner will be waiting for us at Guaymos ten days from now. But I'm getting ahead of the story.

"McCord and his men were to provide me protection. You know they are fully capable. Well, they are also motivated. Each man who survives the trip gets two thousand in cash when we get to Guaymos. I get all the rest. You see, Fargo, I'm a greedy woman. I didn't want to get only half of the five hundred thousand. I want all of it."

"So, Uncle Felix had to go," Fargo mused.

"Correct. He was a louse, in the first place. The world won't miss the likes of him. Then Uncle Felix mentioned he had written to you. I asked him why he did such a fool thing. He said he had it arranged for the wagon master to provoke McCord and his men into a gunfight and kill them all. During the shootout, Uncle Felix and I would take the statue and ride for Guaymos with you as our protection. He said you could handle any trouble all by yourself. Stupid, isn't it?"

"Damn right. All of a sudden, I don't like Uncle Felix's payment schedule for my services. Getting staked to the ground is worth at least five thousand. So, honey, why didn't you have McCord blow a hole in me four nights ago?"

"Now you're getting ahead of the story. I knew McCord would be waiting for us in Domingo. It just so happened that one of the wagon master's men, Hawk Nose, couldn't take his eyes off me. I don't have to tell you how I got him to desert the wagons. Believe me, it was easy and fast. He left during the night and rode for Domingo to tell McCord the plan had changed, that he was to intercept the wagon train the night before it got to Domingo. For his services rendered, Hawk Nose was cut in on the deal.

"I laid awake that night listening for McCord. I never heard their approach. Neither did the wagon master's guard. McCord came in Indian fashion, with his horse's hooves bound with strips of blanket so they wouldn't be heard. Clever, wouldn't you say?"

"I've done it several times. What happened?"

"When I heard the guard gasp, I knew McCord had arrived. Later I saw the man's throat had been slashed. I brought my pistol out from under my pillow, aimed it at Uncle Felix's head, then waited for a shot before pulling the trigger. About a dozen shots were fired, almost simultaneously. The sleeping people never had a chance. The men went first, then the hysterical women and their kids. Unfortunately, it had to be that way.

"We rode into Domingo, scattered and killed some of the people, and pilfered the statuette. No problems. One of McCord's men locked the priest in a room. The priest had no idea what was going on.

"On the way in to Domingo, I decided you might spoil things. At the time I really didn't know what Uncle Felix had put in that letter to you. It was possible you knew more than he told me you did. I couldn't risk you being on our trail. Anything could happen."

"You were right," he mused. "It has."

"I told McCord I would stay behind for one day to watch for you and see what I could learn regarding your intentions. McCord and the Texicans were to ride for Guaymos. At some point, McCord's choice, they were to divide. The group with the statue were to angle west and drift south for Guaymos, while the other group headed southeast. If the southeast group didn't see me within three days, they were to turn and ride for Las Rocas and link up with the others. Everybody, myself included, would meet here.

"Then you showed up only a few hours after we

stole Our Lady. You know what happened after that. I had to catch up with you and divert your attention to the southeastern group. It was pure luck when I spotted the unshod hoofprints. At the same time, I conveniently discovered my bracelet in the sand.

"Like yourself, I had no idea a sandstorm would arrive that night. Not that it mattered, because I planned to sneak away and ride ahead anyhow. I had to get to them. We were getting too far away from the other group. I found them camped out less than two miles from where I left you sound asleep. I rode back and got in my bedroll. You know the rest."

"Not quite," Fargo replied. "Why did you come back? And why didn't McCord and the others leave me dead when they had the chance? Why did you ride at the rear of the column? Why a lot of weird things?"

"I stayed back because you're a resourceful man, obviously a survivor. Uncle Felix couldn't have made a more excellent choice. It was always possible that you would somehow manage to get your hands free. Like I said, you're clever, Fargo. It was necessary to leave doubt about me in your mind. Things changed when the Mexicans came. We needed all the guns we had. So I briefly exposed myself, then got back in line, hopefully to confuse you. When Las Rocas came into sight, I made my position known. McCord didn't kill you because I warned him not to harm you."

"Oh? And why would you turn nice all of a sudden? Is it my eyes?"

"No, although they are fascinating. It was something else about you."

"Such as?"

"What I saw while sitting on the boulder at the spring."

"I'm thirsty. Why don't you go fetch me a dipper of water."

73

Marie laughed. "No, you just think you're thirsty. In about an hour you will know true thirst."

Fargo mentally prepared himself for what he believed she had in mind.

Marie struck a match and Fargo stared at her intently. She was fully dressed and wore two holstered six-guns with matching bandoliers that hid her heavy breasts. The bullwhip was coiled around her left shoulder. He watched her light the candle, which was jammed down in the mouth of a bottle, and place the bottle on the ground at his groin.

Marie smiled wickedly and said, "It's show time, Mr. Fargo. I promise that you have the best seat in the house."

"Uh, huh," he grunted, "I bet I do."

"Too bad there's no music, but I'll make do."

Marie fell into a relaxed pose. She stood six or so feet back from the ankle stakes. Fast as greased lightning the woman drew both six-guns and leveled the barrels between Fargo's eyes.

"Bang, bang," she cried, twirled the weapons expertly, and dropped them back in their holsters. "Pretty fancy, wouldn't you agree?"

"Yep. Best fast draw I've seen in quite a spell. How are you when facing a gunslinger? That's the acid test, you know. A dusty street at sundown separates the men from the boys, and girls."

Marie laughed. "That's my dream, Fargo. One of these days I'll find out."

He watched her unbuckle the gun belt and lower it to the ground. The bandoliers lowered next, then the bullwhip. She removed her boots and set them aside, then started undoing the buttons on her blouse. She kept her eyes on his and pursed her lips provocatively while drawing her arms out of the sleeves.

The faint glow of the candlelight emphasized the smooth curvature of her grapefruit-sized breasts, kissed off the peaks of the large nipples, and embellished the remarkable silver-dollar circles from which they protruded.

Using the blouse as a fan-veil, she covered one breast, then the other, then both, and finally tossed it toward her boots. She kept her eyes fixed on his as she removed the wide sash belt that held up her riding skirt. Marie bent at the waist to work the skirt down over her hips. Her breasts hung heavily and swayed as she drew the skirt down until a patch of dark pubic hair appeared. There she stopped, stood upright, and turned her shapely buttocks to him. Looking over her shoulder, she tensed her fanny muscles. When she did, the skirt fell to the ground. She shot Fargo a quick wink that might have said, "How about that for control, Fargo?" A thin chain made of silver encircled her waist, held up in place only by her hips.

She kept her back to him as she stepped from the blouse crumpled around her feet and ankles. She kicked the garment toward the boots and blouse. As she again bent from the waist, this time to touch her toes, her sultry gaze stayed fixed on his eyes. Captured in the candlelight, the perfectly symmetrical cheeks of her lovely rump rose and broadened into twin mounds that would excite any man. She reached back and slowly spread the cheeks. The pubic hair parted, and her lower charms glistened in the glow of the tiny flame licking up from directly below the erotic pose.

She half-turned and presented her profile. Smiling naughtily, she tilted her head downward, brought one hand under her hair, which flowed down to her shoulder blades, and placed the other near the top of her breastbone. Maintaining the sensual pose, she pushed her hair up over her head and let it fall along the left side of her face. At the same time her other hand slid down between the breasts, over the slightly rounded belly, and into the curly pubic hair.

Marie turned to face him. The silver chain looped down in front, and at the bottom of it dangled a silver medallion. For the first time he saw her shapely body from the front and knew why it had tantalized Boston's finest. Her breasts complimented her broad shoulders, made her softly rounded belly more alluring, and definitely promised that she would be irresistible and well worth investigating.

Pouting, she fondled her breasts, wet her forefinger and thumb, and teased her nipples to stand proud and erect.

Fargo willed himself to think about rocks, trees, cold water, bullets—anything to help take his mind off her. But try as he might to keep it from happening, his organ seemed to have a lustful mind of its own. It rose slowly until it stood full length, blotted his view of the candle's flame, and cast a shadow up his muscled body.

She said, "Too bad you can't see what I'm seeing. Its shadow covers that door. Amazing, Fargo. God has blessed you amply. I intend to gorge myself on that mighty endowment. But first, I'm going to get your full attention and make you break out in a heavy sweat. I like my men sweaty. Monroe sweated best of all."

He watched her retrieve the bullwhip and swing it out to uncoil. With her eyes locked on his, she snapped the tip of the whip several times on the ground and in the air around her. While the graceful half-loops and soft clackings of the long whip and its dangerous tiny tip were done without flaw, Fargo knew the woman was simply warming up.

Without warning the whip's full length came out of a wide loop and flew out straight as an Apache arrow as it floated over him and fell gently down his body. The cruel tip lay on the ground somewhere above his head. She snaked the whip down his body until the tip rested on his left eye. Her wrist barely flicked and the tip hopped to his right eye. He watched and felt it lower and stop on his lips. Suddenly, it jumped to his left nipple, flipped over on the right one, paused, and crept to lay on his navel. Smiling, she drew the tip to the base of his organ and paused again.

"Tickles doesn't it, Fargo?" she asked smugly. A hint of a smile appeared on her lips as she said, "You came in search of a statue, but I found one between your legs. Jewel-encrusted, no, but capable of bringing riches far greater than those on her crown. You see, Fargo, women idolize statues such as yours. Women will gladly open up their treasure chests and let you take all you want. In a word, Fargo, you're a once-in-a-lifetime prize."

Fargo wasn't at all amused by her fancy act with the bullwhip, or all her talk about statues of flesh, treasure chests, and prizes. "You've made your point," he said. "I'm still thirsty, though."

The tip instantly flew back to the ground at her feet. She moved the whip's leather handle back and forth, aligning the length properly. Suddenly, her hand carved figure eights in the air, then jerked down and exploded the tip in a series of loud cracks. For her finale, she popped the donkey on the ass. Fur flew. The little beast of burden kicked, tried to break loose from its tether, and brayed painfully when it could not.

"Marie, you're a cruel bitch," Fargo admonished.

"I know," she replied, and popped the animal on the rump again.

Fargo didn't see her hand move, but he heard the tip crack by his left ear and felt the dirt it kicked loose from the ground. Steeling himself for a mistake on her part, he watched the figure eight and downward yank. The sharp crack temporarily deafened his right ear. Moving quickly now, she cracked the whip just above his left eye, then over the right. Almost simultaneously it cracked close enough to his left nipple that he felt the air disturbed. Loud sounds tingled his other nipple, his navel, left and right big toes, both knees. In rapid succession she cracked it twice on each side of the bottle holding the candle. He felt the sudden movements of the air high in his groin area, then noticed the candle's flame flicker. Still, without expression he stared into her eyes.

She drew the whip back to her after its last dance around the bottle. "Fargo, you're a cool son of a bitch. I'll say that much for you. Look down your body. Look at all that sweat rolling off it. You haven't seen anything yet. Suck in your gut, Fargo, here it comes."

He gazed down his muscled torso and saw she was correct.

As he looked at his sweat, the tip cracked again, this time snuffing out the flame, casting the space in total darkness. Almost immediately he felt the last foot or so of the whip's end coil gently around his organ at its base. As though by magic the coil stroked up its length and eased off the crest. Hair cascaded down onto his upper thighs and all around his manhood. He felt her warm moist lips encircle the crown, tighten, and push the foreskin down. Her tongue explored him. Slowly, her lips lowered until her mouth and soft throat could take no more. He listened to her mews and gurgles as the lips stroked up and down, trying with each downward movement to capture one new inch.

While gulping on it, she struck a match to relight the candle. He saw that she'd moved the bottle next to his right hip and that she now knelt between his parted thighs to suck. With the candle lit, she and the room took on a new forms. In the soft glow, her bobbing head created a most erotic scene.

Her lips slid up slowly and smacked when they left the peak. She parted her hair and looked into his eyes. "Tell me that wasn't the best you ever had and I'll set you free, Fargo."

"I've had better," he lied. "Up in Colorado there's a she-bear—"

"Piss on you," she quipped testily to cut him short. "We both know you were struggling to hold back the flow."

"I'm still thirsty," he replied dryly.

She cupped a breast. "I know you would dearly love to quench that thirst on this, or . . ." Her other had dipped to her love mound. The long middle finger pressed along the length of her lower lips, spreading them apart. "But, as badly as I want your face and mouth on both, I wouldn't dare accommodate you. You'd bite me."

"No, I wouldn't," he answered with a hint of a lie in the tone. "Trust me."

Marie laughed and moved the candle next to his chest. She inched forward on her knees, bent at the waist, and put her palms on the ground on each side of his chest. Her eyes looked up at his chiseled face. She smiled and ran her tongue around her luscious lips, whispered, "No, Fargo, I trust only myself."

As she lowered her open mouth to his left nipple, her twin peaks dragged across his muscular abdomen. After a few teasing seconds, her breasts pressed against him. They were pillowy, warm, and moist with perspiration. Her soft tongue caressed his erect nipples, licked both, then lapped all around them. She buried her face against the right one and sucked hard. Again he heard her mews and gurgles of delight.

Her wet lips and busy tongue moved down his flat belly and stopped on his navel. As she probed its depth and swished her tongue around the inside, her palms went to his pectoral muscles. They felt, squeezed, explored, patted, and traced circles. He noticed her breathing had quickened, and he felt her hot breath on his navel and abdomen. Her right hand moved down. The long fingers curled around the throbbing shaft, stroked slowly a few times, then uncurled after a hard grip.

Sitting back, she whispered, "Jesus, Fargo, you taste as good as you look. At another time in another place . . ." she began. Her wonderment trailed off.

He watched her stand and move to kneel above his head. She was holding her long hair back when she bent and wet his left eye with her tongue. Moving to the right eye, she kissed it, slid her tongue to his left ear, and probed the inside, nibbled on the lobe.

Fargo tried to suppress a low moan. She heard it, shifted to the other ear, and massaged it with her lips and tongue. Fargo's hands clenched and opened. He fought to pull a stake out of the ground but could not.

"Drives you wild, doesn't it, Fargo? Well, that's the whole idea. The best part, the serious part, is yet to come." She glanced between his legs. "That's what I want. I intend to have my fill of it."

Fargo watched her stand and straddle him at the waist. She reached behind and gripped his length, raised a knee high, and positioned his blood-swollen crown for insertion. Lowering slowly, she fed it in and gasped, "Oh, God . . . oh, God! This is wonderful. So big . . . so damn big."

He felt her soft lower lips plunge downward. "Aaayy-eeiiii," she shrieked. "Jesus, oh, yes, yes, yes . . . Sweet Jesus, that's powerful. Oh, my God, yes!"

Her hips rotated, squatted, rose quickly, and shoved down. Fargo strained on the stakes. Marie whimpered, "Deeper . . . deeper. I want it all. Help me, goddammit, help me get it all."

Fargo willed himself not to move. He watched her tits bounce as she romped, squealing, "Oh, goddamn,

goddamn . . . yes, yes, yes . . this is soooo good."

Her head tilted back and she cupped her perfect breasts, squeezed them, and gasped, "Where . . . oh, where, have you been all my life? Oh, God . . . it's so filling . . . so hard, so long!"

Marie Mercier's head snapped forward and her hands dropped to his pectoral muscles. He saw a wildness flashing in her widened eyes, a maniacal expression on her face, gritted teeth behind her parted, drawn lips. The woman was clearly approaching the zenith of her sexual madness.

Again Fargo tried to force his mind to see and think about ice-cold water, jagged rocks, blizzards—anything to deny her the pleasure of feeling him erupt—and failed.

He knew she could feel the tremors signaling his building explosion. She shifted into a furious rocking motion, back and forth in wild slippery jerks, as though her crotch was fanning it, demanding the gusher to spew forth. "Come on . . . let it go!" she screamed. "Don't fight it, Fargo!"

She anticipated it, dug her fingernails into his chest, and clawed till blood appeared. "Now, Fargo," she screamed.

He felt her contractions begin as she threw her head back and gasped, "Oh, Jesus . . . sweet Jesus, yes."

Fargo erupted.

Marie sucked in a breath.

She squatted, reached behind, and parted the cheeks of her rump to make all the room possible, pushed down and fused her stretched lips to his mighty base.

Squirming to help milk the last drop from him, she whimpered, "Oh, God, I'm on fire inside . . . so full. Nice, nice . . . more, Fargo, more . . . fill me to overflowing."

She was calm now. Her face glowed with rapture. A pretty smile met his gaze. He watched her breasts rise and fall with each exhausted breath. Rising, she said, "Mister, I might not kill you, after all."

"Huh. Damn near did. Honey, you're crazy. How many men have you left dead in bed?"

Marie stepped away. "Odd that you would ask. Four to be exact. All from Boston's upper crust. Older men trying to act like they were young again. A pity, in a way. At least they died with happy faces."

Fargo watched her dress, strap on the gun belt, and pick up the bullwhip. With the bottle in hand she turned to leave. "Honey, my throat is still dry," he reminded.

"No water, Fargo. Not yet, anyway. My romping you wasn't done out of pure lust, although that played a part of it."

"In what?" he asked quickly.

She walked to the door before answering, "I want to keep you weak as a kitten, Fargo. Delilah whacked off Samson's hair. A few more of these escapades can serve the same purpose. Lack of food and water simply helps cause a man to lose his strength faster. I'll be back. Next time I'll reduce you to a blubbering idiot."

Fargo heard the door grate open then close. He stared up into the darkness and thought of many things, none having anything to do with sex, all concerning violence. She's a bloodthirsty bitch, mean and unusually cruel. It can only end one way for her—and Mad Jack McCord too. Sooner or later I'll get an ankle or wrist loose. When I do . . .

7

Sleep came hard to Skye Fargo. The inability to move naturally became more than a nuisance. He tried straining on the ropes, lifting his back from the ground, and holding it up till his lungs screamed for air—anything and everything to tire himself, to enter exhaustion and sleep a deep sleep. All he got for his efforts was a heavily sweating body.

Catching his wind between tuggings, he thought of Marie and Mad Jack, and of how he'd eradicate them from the face of the earth. While killing both would be a pleasure as well as a necessity, Fargo's ordeal made him want see her suffer more than Mad Jack. He'd bring a fast end to McCord, but Marie? No, she needed to know pain first.

The room was exceedingly hot. Fargo wondered how the donkey survived. He wondered how he survived. Neither of them could reach the water. Fargo listened to the little animal jerk at its tether to break free and get at the pail.

"Forget it, donkey," Fargo yelled. "Like me, you can't get away."

Still the donkey yanked on its rope.

Much later the moon rose and crept high enough for its beams to paint Las Rocas in bright whites and black shadows. Fargo watched the metamorphosis through the cracks in the boards of the front wall where the donkey stood. It was something to do.

Shafts of light diffused by the scant openings stabbed down on the ground to Fargo's left. As the moon rose higher, the crisp beams inched toward him. He watched one move slowly across his chest, onto the ground, over his right arm, and creep toward the crack. During its silent, slow movement he finally drifted to sleep.

Fargo's wild-creature hearing snapped his eyes open. He glanced to the cracks. Dawn was breaking. Listening keenly, he focused his attention on the wide side door and wished he could see the other one. Whatever had awakened him didn't come from either door. He looked up at the almost invisible rafters. The soft sounds of bare feet padded on the floor above. A female?

He continued to listen, remaining alert. Soon the hard sounds of men moving about filtered down from above. They're stirring. Fargo wondered who he would see next, Marie or one of the others? It made no difference as long as they brought water.

Before long, sunlight spilled through the cracks. A thud on the floor above told him an empty whiskey bottle had been dropped. Boots stomped on the wood. Somebody is getting into his boots. The boots clomped across the floor. A door grated open but wasn't closed. Fargo heard bedsprings squeak, as though someone had rolled over.

The muted curses shouted by a man penetrated the thick wood at which Skye Fargo's eyes stared. "Get out of that bed an' go get me a bottle!" It sounded like J.T. "While you're at it, wake up somebody an' tell 'em to fix me breakfast. Goddammit, bitch, I told you to git. Now do it or I'll beat you. Move!"

Fargo heard her leave the bed and shuffle out of the room. Again the springs squeaked.

A mixture of sounds and voices told Fargo that J.T.'s woman had indeed roused others from sleep.

That activity denied him hearing the woman return with the whiskey for J.T. Fargo lost interest.

He looked outside through the cracks. The *zócalo* beyond the gurgling stream was deserted. He decided the people were too afraid to come out of their small abodes to fill their water buckets and jars from the communal well. By stretching his neck upward, he brought part of the mission's front entrance into view. He noticed the big wood door was open. Nobody came or went through it. They were too scared to go to the mission and pray.

The door in the end wall grated. Fargo tried to look above his head. A man's voice—he believed it was Sawtooth's—growled, "Touch them ropes an' I'll lay your throat open."

The door swung shut.

Chachona stepped into view. She held a bowl of something steamy. Putting a finger to her lips, she knelt at his waist and whispered, "Don't try to talk. I've brought you soup."

He nodded. Chachona dipped a spoon in the bowl and began feeding him. As she did, she told him, "Fargo, these are mean *hombres*." She paused to glance at the ceiling. "Dolores Sánchez told me they are going to kill you. But not right away. They will do it before they leave Las Rocas."

After licking the spoon he asked, "You know when they're going?"

"Dolores said tomorrow. The white woman—she's the *jefa*—wanted to go today, but the others said no, that they want to have more fun first. So she said okay. That's what Dolores told me."

"Where's the statue?"

"I haven't seen it. Nobody has. But all the women I spoke with say they believe it's in the cantina. Two of the Texicans stay there all the time. None of the people are allowed to go inside the cantina. It must be true."

"Will the men of Las Rocas fight?"

"No, *señor*, they are scared. Everybody is afraid. There are no guns in Las Rocas. The *federales* won't let anybody have guns. All the people want, all they pray for, is for these *conchinos* to hurry up and leave. No, the men won't fight."

"Chachona, I want you to learn where they have the statue. It may or may not be in the cantina. Make it your business to find out where it is, and whether or not they are guarding it."

She glanced to the ropes and stakes. "*Señor*, how do you plan to escape?"

He had an idea. "The next time you come with food, bring a knife. Tie it to a thigh, anywhere, but bring it. All I need is to get one hand or foot free." After a brief pause, he added, "One more thing, Chachona. Tell the women not to do anything that will make the Texicans really angry. They must keep them as happy as they can. Tell them to get the men stupid drunk as fast as they can. I mean, keep pouring whiskey down their gullets. Get them drunk and see that they stay drunk. It's important. Think you can do that?"

"Sure. Then what, *señor*?"

"We fetch the statue and get the hell out of Las Rocas."

"You make it sound so easy."

"It will be, if your lady friends help the Texicans pass out."

"I'll tell them."

Chachona stood and gazed down his muscled body. He watched her eyes linger between his parted thighs. Glancing back to his face, she smiled.

Fargo tried to take her gaze and mind off his crotch. "Next time you come, bring me a drink of water."

She glanced to the water pail. Reaching for the bucket, she said, "I'm sorry, *señor*, I thought you were getting water."

"No, no," he quickly said to stop her. "I don't want any of that water. It's been tainted. A man could die if he drank from that bucket."

The donkey brayed.

Chachona shrugged, glanced at his groin, then moved for the door. Within seconds she was back. This time she didn't look anywhere but at his groin. As she bent over, her heavy breasts swung low and he felt her hand lift and bounce his organ, as though weighing it. *"Qué grande,"* she muttered.

He watched her walk away and heard the door open and close. He went back to looking through the cracks and talking to the donkey. The higher the sun got, the more uncomfortable the big room became. By noon, Fargo was sweating profusely. The Texicans whooped and hollered, shot their pistols, flung empty whiskey bottles from the balcony to splash in the stream below. Fargo nodded and smiled each time another bottle splashed. At the rate the *señoritas* were pouring liquor down them, they'll all be dead drunk in no time.

In mid afternoon he was gazing through a crack and saw a chubby *señora* with a water jug come to the well. After pausing to look nervously at the balcony, she set the jug down and started hauling in the well rope.

One of the men fired his pistol. The slug chewed into the jug, shattering it. The woman let go of the well rope. Two more shots were fired. The bullets struck the ground on either side of the terrified woman. Laughter erupted on the balcony.

The woman started running. Rapid fire from several pistols kicked up geysers of soil behind her. When she stumbled and fell, the slugs caught up with her. The woman did not get up. Fargo looked away.

The revelry on the balcony continued throughout the afternoon. Fargo was amazed by the Texicans' ability to hold their liquor. He thought that by now all should be falling-down drunk. As though on cue, he heard them staggering down the stairs and across the bridge. Through the cracks he watched them move clumsily onto the plaza, where they reeled, stumbled, and fell, laughing all the time, firing their pistols wildly. Each held a bottle in his free hand. Somehow they managed to stagger or crawl to the well. Fargo counted eight Texicans sitting on the ground with their backs against the well. One by one they drank themselves into a stupor and slumped over. He wondered where Marie, Mad Jack McCord, Hawk Nose, and Sawtooth were.

Night fell and he was still wondering. When the moon came up, he watched the Texicans' *señoritas*, all armed with bottles of whiskey, go to the well. Clearly, they were intent on fulfilling their role to keep the men drunk. Fargo couldn't keep from grinning as he watched the women stick the bottles in the men's mouths.

The ladies stood in a group while talking, then parted and heaved their men up. Fargo watched them stagger and reel under the almost deadweight of the drunks as the women maneuvered them onto the bridge and out of his sight. Above him, he heard doors open and close, boots shuffle on wood floors, bedsprings rebel loudly. The women had performed well.

Not long thereafter, he heard the door open gently. He waited and watched for Chachona to arrive. Instead, he saw a shadowy form go to the donkey and untie its tether. The dark form walked on the far side of the donkey as it was led to the wide door. Fargo stayed silent, watched the door open only far enough to allow the donkey and person passage. The moonbeams cast the alley in black shadows. He couldn't make out who was taking the animal. The wide door closed. He listened to the donkey and whoever took it walk away.

After a minute or so, he heard the donkey walking across the bridge. Both the donkey and the nocturnal visitor hurried past the cracks too fast for Fargo to tell who was leading it.

He waited.

Within half an hour, the horseman, now trailing the donkey, passed again, this time headed in the opposite direction. While they moved beyond the cracks quickly, he saw something different about the donkey. Fargo forced himself to recall what he'd glimpsed. The donkey was rigged to pack something, something large enough to . . . The statue? Yes, that's it. Somebody is going for the statue. Who? To take it where? Why? The more he thought on it, the fewer answers he got.

About midnight, he heard a horse come onto the plaza. Fargo stared through the cracks. The horseman rode next to the far bank of the stream, headed in the direction from which the rider had trailed the donkey earlier, only now there was no donkey. Fargo still couldn't see who rode on the horse.

Shortly, the rider returned on foot. Fargo strained to see through the cracks, but all he managed was a fleeting glimpse of the person, too little and too fast for him to determine who. He did hear bootsteps on the bridge, then on the stairs. In the stillness of the night, Fargo heard a chair being moved on the balcony. Fargo reckoned the man was seating himself to have a late-night drink or two before going to bed. During the next hour, he heard the chair grate on the tile floor several times and the restless man move about on the balcony. He wished Chachona would make her appearance.

The moon lowered. Fargo lay in near total darkness and stared upward, his ears tuned to the balcony. The person was still up there, restless as before. The chair would grate on the tile. He'd listen to the person patrol the balcony from one end to the other, come back and sit, get up and start pacing again. Only now the bootsteps seemed to have a drunken clumsiness to them. Fargo decided it might be Mad Jack up there. The man had stolen the statue, Fargo decided, then got to thinking about it.

He heard the chair crash on the tile, then a table when it fell over. He listened to the man crawl on the balcony. Once again the night fell deathly silent. But not for long. Fargo heard someone stumbling down the steps leading to the door above his head. The door was shoved open. Fargo rolled his eyes back, now knowing he would not see Chachona.

He smelled her scent before she lurched across the room to stand, swaying drunkenly over his head. "Well, Fargo," Marie slurred, "I see you're all laid out and ready for me."

"Water," he moaned feebly.

She moved to stand at his waist. "You don't get any water," she snarled.

He could barely see her, but he heard her garments fall onto the ground. She got down on her hands and knees and began crawling, feeling her way to between his legs. He felt her hair drag up his thigh, her fingers go around his limp length and lift it from the ground. "Fargo, you're big even when it's asleep. I'll change that."

He felt her lips on him. She shoved her head down hard, sucked harder. But she was too drunk to keep her rhythm or balance. Marie fell forward. Giggling, she tried to find it again. "Slips don't count, Fargo."

He noticed her words came with difficulty. Clearly, Marie was on the verge of passing out.

Her naked body dragged over his. She was trying to stand and kept collapsing onto him. She'd grab his body, dig fingernails in his flesh, grunt as she pushed up, then squeal when her soused brain made her lose her equilibrium and she tumbled askew. He knew she'd never straddle him.

Grumbling under her breath, Marie struggled to get into position where she could mount him. She began by lying across his abdomen and shoving on the ground with her feet until her smooth ass rested on hard stomach. "Feel that? I'm getting close."

Grunting, she straddled him at the waist with her back to his face. On wobbly knees she crept forward. He felt her pubic hair brush over his just before she fell forward and grabbed his outstretched knees. She rested a few seconds with her rump raised high, poised to come down on him. It was a clumsy position, one that amused Fargo. He wondered what was going on inside her muddled brain.

She sat up suddenly and moved back onto his abdomen. Grabbing his organ with both hands, she started stroking. "Get hard, damn you," she demanded.

He knew it wouldn't accommodate what she had in mind. Still she tried. He felt her inch down again until her moist love tunnel met the base of his swelling length. Her hands fumbled and found his kneecaps.

She tried several times to position her bottom on his crest, but it was a futile effort. "Damn," she muttered. "Looks like you could help. Goddammit, Fargo, try."

"Water," he moaned.

Marie turned and slapped his face. "You go to hell," she yelled. Rising to stand wobbly, she cursed, "Bastard! I don't need you!"

Fargo watched her vague form totter toward the open door. On the way to it she repeated, "I don't need you," and added, "I'm gonna kill you, Fargo. Hear that? I said I was gonn—"

He heard her body fall onto the stairs. Marie didn't get up. She was out, her brain probably swimming in circles.

What next? Fargo wondered.

8

Skye Fargo angled his face toward the cracks in the wall and watched dawn break while he listened to several roosters crowing outside. Closer to him he could hear the soft sounds Marie made as she slept where she fell in the doorway.

Chachona was in the room before he heard her. This time she carried both water and food, tortillas, half a chicken, and a cup of saffron rice. He motioned for her to bend an ear to his lips.

"Did you bring the knife?" he whispered. When she nodded, he told her to put the food down and cut the rope holding his right hand to the stake.

Free at last, he rolled onto his left side and gestured for her to give him the knife. Moving quickly, he severed the other three ropes, then sat and gulped down the water first. The chicken disappeared in four bites. He dumped the rice onto two of the tortillas, folded them, then devoured both in seconds.

While he wolfed down the food, he looked at Marie sprawled in the doorway and on the lower steps. She wore neither the gun belt nor the silver waist chain.

Chachona watched him stand and stretch the kinks from his powerful body. He nodded toward the doorway. Looking down on Marie, he waited for one of the roosters to crow and mask any accidental sound he or Chachona made. When one accommodated him, they stepped over Marie's sleeping body and eased up the stairs. On the top landing, he whispered to Chachona, "The first thing I must do is find out where they have my clothes and guns. Do you know where they are?"

Chachona shook her head.

Fargo glanced about the narrow hallway and saw four closed doors. He opened the first one and peered inside. A naked Texican and two equally nude *señoritas* lay sleeping on the bed. He didn't see any of his gear. They moved across the hall and he gently opened another door. In the room a Texican and a girl were asleep, the man snoring in alcoholic blubbers. Not seeing his clothes or guns, Fargo withdrew and stepped to the next door.

Pushing it open quietly, he looked inside. Sawtooth was lying faceup, snoring softly, while two women lay on either side of him. Both women were wide awake. Fargo lifted a finger to his lips. One of the women kept darting her eyes to her left. He realized she wanted him to follow her gaze. He did and saw his clothes piled on the seat of a straight-back chair. The woman raised her head from the pillow and nodded toward the opposite side of the small room. Fargo saw his gun belt and Sharps on the floor in the corner.

Turning to Chachona, the Trailsman winked at her and indicated for her to stay put. He kept his eyes fastened on Sawtooth as he eased his way to the weapons. He picked up his gun and moved softly to the other side of the room. Fargo's eyes told the women not to move or make a sound.

He motioned for Chachona to shut the door, then stepped to the straight-back chair and pulled on his clothes. Strapping on his gun belt, he whispered to the two wide-eyed females, "When we leave here, I want you to be quiet. Get out of the building, then run as fast as you can to tell the people to stay inside their homes. Spread the word quickly. Tell them it's important to keep their doors and windows closed and barred tight. There might be a lot of running and shooting this morning. I don't want anybody to get hurt. *Comprenden*?"

They both showed quizzical expressions to Chachona. *"Ellas no comprenden, señor"* she whispered. "I will tell them what you said."

While she was translating his warning, Fargo stepped to the door and glanced about the shadowy hallway. When he heard Chachona finish, he gestured for all to leave.

He let the two females go first. After watching them clear the hallway, he motioned Chachona back into the room and closed the door. He looked down into her curious dark eyes and whispered, "This is going to be a bloody day in Las Rocas." She nodded. He continued. "Do you know how to handle a gun?" Again Chachona nodded. This time she reached for the rifle. He drew it away from her grasp. "You sure?"

"Sí," she whispered. "I shoot straight, *señor*."

She had said it so emphatically that he believed her. He gave her the Sharps and a handful of cartridges. "There are still ten of them alive. And we still have to locate that statue. Do you understand, Chachona?"

"Sí," she replied without hesitation, and pocketed the extra bullets.

"Good," he said. "If we are lucky, we will find it before anyone wakes up. If some of them are guarding it, we can hope they're sound asleep. Maybe, just maybe, we can sneak Our Lady out of Las Rocas without awakening anyone. All we need is a good head start."

"The cantina?" she queried.

"No. First we saddle up. Take me to my horse. You do know where it is?"

"It's in the corral with their horses. When I saw your big pinto, I knew you were here." Hooking a thumb over her shoulder, she added, "The corral is that way, next to the south wall, by the gate."

"By the way, Chachona, what brought you to this town?"

The abrupt change in subject jarred her. She seemed uneasy when explaining, "To visit my grandmother. I heard she was sick and maybe dying. I came to see her."

"And?"

"She's all right. She was ill, but she has recovered now. Shall we go now?"

He nodded, opened the door, and stepped out into the hallway. Within seconds they were on the balcony. Fargo paused to let the first rays of the morning sun smack his face, then he looked at the empty bottles littering the tile deck and shook his head. He led her down the stairs and onto the plaza.

Chachona pointed toward the narrow street that led to the plaza from the south. "The horses are down that street, *señor*."

Following her point, he asked, "And the cantina?"

She looked north and pointed to another narrow, dusty street. "It's in there. A big place. Larger than the cantina in Domingo. Glass windows and everything. Even a mirror. You can't see the cantina from here."

He looked that way, then muttered, "Rotten luck. Couldn't be worse. Cantina one way, horse another. Is there a back door?"

"I haven't been inside, so I wouldn't know. There must be a back way, though."

"I need to know, be sure. You go check, then catch up with me at the corral."

"*Sí, señor.*" She turned around and went on her way, throwing him a smile as she started running.

Fargo glanced about the deserted square for signs of people who might be too curious to stay indoors as ordered. The roosters had stopped crowing. The sun seemed eager to watch the events of this day in Las Rocas. It was now peeking between the mission and a row of connected homes. Seeing nobody, Fargo headed for the street leading to the corral.

The dirt street was desolate and eerily silent except for one of the roosters and several hens that hurried away in advance of his approach. Passing a door in one of the abodes, he saw it was slightly ajar; dark eyes, wide with fear, stared at him through the crack. He paused to wink at them, then pulled the door shut and moved on.

A happy smile spread across Skye's face when he rounded the corner and saw the Ovaro standing proudly, his big black eyes fixed on him, his ears perked, keenly alert. The stallion came to stand at the railings. It was as though the big pinto knew trouble was in the air.

Fargo rubbed the Ovaro's forehead and patted his powerful neck before going through the railings. Tack lined one of the top railings. He found Mad Jack's gear, took it to the big dun, and saddled it for Chachona to ride.

After saddling the pinto, Fargo selected a well-fed burro. He glanced about the corral and saw a pack he felt was ideal for the statue. He led the furry burro to the pack and strapped it onto the little beast of burden. While he worked, he saw Chachona sprint around the corner and hurry to the corral.

Out of breath, she gasped, "They have a back door. It's wide open. After hearing loud snores, I looked in. Two of the men were sleeping on the floor. The front door is open too."

Fargo nodded. He reviewed what he knew; alcohol had taken its toll on Marie, who was still sleeping in the doorway; Sawtooth was in a similar state; two others were in rooms off the hallway; and this pair was asleep in the cantina. He wondered where the other four were. "Anybody else in there with them? Women?"

Her head shook. "No, *señor*, only the men."
Chachona's next observance drew his eyes off the burro.
"*Señor*, I think I saw Our Lady in the cantina."

"Why do you say 'think'?"

"It was dark in there. I saw what might be Our
Lady standing on top of the bar. I said I thought it was
her, because it's about as tall as the statue. I couldn't
be sure because they had it draped with a *sarape*."
Chachona shrugged.

Fargo nodded toward the saddled dun. "Your
mount," he said. "All ready to ride."

Chachona glanced at the horse, then shot Fargo a
pleased wink. Stroking the rifle barrel, she said, "I
ride well too."

Fargo grinned at her. "I'm sure of it," he replied.
"Get your horse and let's see how quiet we can be
going to the cantina."

She grabbed the saddle horn, hiked a bare foot
high, and pulled herself up in the saddle. Fargo handed
her a handful of bullets for the Sharps, then went to
open the gate. After tying his rope to the burro, he
paid out enough length for easy trailing and secured
the rest around his saddle horn. Mounting, he nodded
toward the gate.

Coming onto the dusty street, he motioned for
Chachona to come alongside him. He said, "Contrary
to popular belief, I don't have eyes in the back of my
head. So, your job is to help protect my back. When
we get to the square, I'll watch the front and sides.
You keep an eye out behind us. If you see any movement, tell me but keep the dun walking. You're going
to show me the way to that back door. Understand?"

Nodding, she replied, "*Comprendo.*"

"Fine. Fall in behind me and stay close to the front
wall."

He moved the Ovaro to the wall and watched all
along both sides of the street. As he neared the far

corner, he halted and turned in the saddle to give final instructions.

Chachona was watching behind them, as he had ordered. "Ssspptt," he hissed to get her attention. Her head whipped forward. He watched her eyes dart left and right, then stare at his. Fargo suppressed a forming chuckle and said, "Crossing the *zócalo* is the dangerous part. Keep those eyes and ears open. Be alert. Trouble always happens fast. Ready?"

When she gulped and nodded, he grinned, drew the Colt, and nudged the pinto forward at a walk.

Chachona tensed and raised the Sharps, prepared to swing and fire in any direction.

In one fast sweep that missed nothing, Fargo's gaze crossed over the balcony, all along the structure at ground level, then over the mission. All he saw between them and the far side of the plaza were a few chickens near the well. He angled the pinto to pass between the well and mission. As he did, he motioned for Chachona to come ride next to him.

Approaching the well, she came alongside. He asked, "Which way do I—?"

A shot rang through the air.

The bullet whizzed past Fargo's chiseled face by no more than an inch. He dropped from the saddle and rolled for the well. The chickens fled squawking.

The Sharps barked. "On the balcony," Chachona cried.

Fargo heard her leave the dun. A split second later she leapt belly-down next to him, and they both squirmed to safety behind the well's rock-and-adobe circular sides. "See who it was?" he asked.

"Her," Chachona answered.

Knowing the shot had knocked all sleepers out of bed, Fargo decided they had less than ten seconds before all hell broke loose. They had to leave the well. As he inched his head out to get a fix on Marie's position, she fired twice. Both slugs kissed off the well.

He drew back and told Chachona, "She can only shoot one of us. When I say go, you run for the mission. I'll roll out on the ground and give her something to worry about."

Chachona's expression told him she didn't think his was such a good idea.

"Don't be afraid. It's me she wants, not you. You'll make it inside."

Chachona hurriedly crossed herself.

Fargo took a firm grip on the Colt's handle, rolled from behind the well, and shouted, "Go!"

In a fraction of the instant Fargo swung around and leveled his gun on Marie Mercier. Both of her six-guns were aimed toward the well. He fired twice. One bullet struck the balcony railing at her waist, ricocheted right, and chewed into the wall behind her. The other bullet simply missed, but not by much. It knocked a chunk out of the wall behind her head.

Marie dropped instantly and crawled across the deck out of sight. Fargo quickly replaced the rounds he spent on Marie, then glanced behind him in time to see Chachona enter the mission.

As he stood, she called out to him. "The back door! Take the street next to the mission!"

Fargo sprinted that way, but the twin geysers of dirt that sprang up close in front of him changed his direction. Both shots came from where he was headed. He angled left, fired twice in the direction of the two shots, and ran for the street leading to the front of the cantina.

He heard Marie yell, "Get him, Mullins, before he gets to that street. Where are you, Alvin?"

"Down here," Alvin's high-pitched voice hollered back.

Fargo glanced over his shoulder. Marie, flanked by

J.T. and Hawk Nose, was running down the staircase. She ran around the corner of the building and disappeared. Alvin crouched on the far side of the stream. Mullins stopped on the bridge and shot twice. The two bullets zinged past Fargo's right ear and slammed into the adobe corner where he ducked.

Fargo looked at the mission's front door to see why Chachona wasn't firing. The Sharps' long barrel appeared in the opening. She commenced shooting. Alvin and J.T. fired back at her. "Good girl," Fargo muttered, turned, and ran down the street.

A nervous Spanish voice shouted through a partly opened door, "Mister! On the roof!"

Fargo instantly fell and swung the Colt up. As he was falling, the man on the roof fired his pistol. The slug tore into the wood door, and the people inside screamed. Fargo squeezed the trigger once. A patch of blood spread across the front of the gunman's checked shirt. The big Texican looked at it as though astonished. With his eyes open in disbelief and his mouth gaping, the fellow plummeted to the ground in front of Fargo and gasped his last breath. Fargo stepped around the body.

"He killed Neil," shouted a man inside the cantina.

That loud announcement told Skye Fargo that the man's partner was stationed at the back door.

Fargo watched both directions while he worked his way along the wall to the glass panes fronting the cantina.

Behind him the Sharps continued to bark. He knew that wouldn't last long. Even as he thought about it, a blistering volley of pistol shots erupted. The Sharps fell silent.

Poised against the wall next to the dirty pane, Fargo glanced up the street toward the square. Mullins leapt around the corner and aimed his six-gun at The Trailsman. Fargo whirled, swung the Colt around, and shot the man. The bullet's impact lifted Mullins off the ground and knocked him backward.

Fargo pressed his back to the wall and reloaded while looking at Mullins' body. It showed no signs of life. When he heard those inside speak in low tones, his attention shifted to the grimy glass panes.

"Harris, this ain't so good," one whined.

"Yeah," Harris agreed. "He's out there, all right. Somebody is at least." His voice strengthened. "That you, Mullins?"

"Yeah, Harris," Fargo answered, muffling his voice with a palm. "I got him. Come out and see for yourselves."

They didn't take his bait. "Like hell," the whiny voice retorted. "You ain't Mullins. Mullins, he can't talk."

Fargo heard their boot steps hurry away from the front of the cantina, then two tables hit the floor. That told him where he would find them.

He backed across the street at an angle where it would be impossible for them to see him, then ran and dived through the glass window. Harris and the other man started shooting.

Fargo rolled toward the bar, shot the gun out of one Texican's hand, and drilled a bullet through the center of the other overturned table.

"I give up," the whiny voice cried. He stood up with his right hand raised, but Fargo saw the man draw with his left. Fargo was too quick for the wounded man, though, and he shot him between the eyes.

Harris' feeble voice mumbled, "Let's make a deal."

Fargo crawled down along the bottom of the bar until Harris' prone form came into view. But Harris, too, had his gun drawn and was ready to fire when Fargo squeezed off a shot. Harris instantly grew still as the red patch of blood seeped across his chest.

Rising, Fargo muttered, "I don't take prisoners, and

I don't cut deals with thieves and murderers." While glancing about to spot the statue, he reloaded the Colt. He didn't see it on top of the bar or out in the room. He leaned over the top of the bar and looked, but it wasn't there.

The sound of movement beyond the closed back door caught his attention. He glanced through the short passageway that led to the back door. The storeroom door was in the wall on his left. He eased toward it and was about to open it when the hinges on the back door squalled raucously as it was jerked open.

Alvin hesitated a fraction too long in pulling the trigger, but not long enough to keep from firing the shot. During the blink, Fargo jerked open the storeroom door. Alvin's bullet chewed through the wood and buzzed harmlessly past Fargo's left shoulder.

Before Alvin could fire again, Fargo pumped two bullets into the skinny man's heart. He watched Alvin drop, then muttered, "Too bad, Alvin. You had the right idea, only in the wrong place at the wrong time."

Fargo reloaded during the brief moment it took him to look into the storeroom. The statue stood among wood crates filled with bottles of *cerveza*. As Chachona had reported, a colorful *sarape* was draped over it.

He stooped to clear the top of the door and stepped inside. Reaching over the crates, he yanked off the *sarape*.

An eighteen-inch-wide log about three feet tall stood there. Fargo chuckled and shook his head. "Hell, I knew it wouldn't be here," he told the fake statuette. "Our Lady isn't anywhere in Las Rocas."

He backed out of the small storage room and left through the cantina's rear entrance. He grimaced at the racket made by the rusty hinges when he shut the door. He looked up and down the dusty back street, then headed for the mission.

As he walked, his eyes scanned the edges of the

103

roofs. Occasionally he glanced over his shoulder to check behind.

A small flock of chickens scattered and ran before him, their cluckings the only sounds he heard.

He wondered how many rounds Chachona had left, if any. He hadn't heard her firing. He hadn't heard any shots since Alvin.

The large white cock in front of Fargo strutted out of the street and headed toward the mission. The rest of the flock hurried to follow it.

Fargo moved alongside the dwellings with the Colt up and ready for action.

When he noticed the chickens flinched and scattered to the left, he halted.

Poised to shoot, he eased the trigger back by a hair's width and held it. The slightest backward pressure would let the hammer fall. He watched and waited.

Three things happened almost simultaneously: he heard the hinges rebel behind him, the muzzle of an Army Colt appeared waist-high at the corner of the street, and the door directly across from where he stood opened.

He tried to look in all three directions at the same time. He glimpsed J.T. dive out of the cantina, wasted a shot on him, then swung around in time to see Hawk Nose peeking around the corner. Fargo forced him back with a shot that knocked a big sliver out of the corner, then began a swing around to confront J.T. again. During the fast movement, his gaze flashed across the open doorway, and he saw an obviously terrified short man waving him inside.

Fargo did not hesitate. It took only two long strides for him to clear the doorway. As he drew his right foot inside, four bullets chewed into the outside wall next to the door. Two other bullets, both fired from the Army Colt, slammed into the door casing.

Fargo shoved the door closed and ordered, "Get out of here. Run out the back way. *Ándale.*"

The man stared at him, answered, *"No comprendo"*

Not one to waste time and not wanting to say it again in Spanish, Fargo dashed to the rear, but found only a solid adobe wall. He quickly turned and aimed his Colt at the front door. He gestured for the man, his wife, and two toddlers to lie on the floor. The chubby woman grabbed both youngsters, shoved them under the bed, and tried to follow. The husband plastered his back to a side wall and began crossing himself. Fargo waited.

But not for long. The door swung in. Fargo applied pressure on the trigger, held it, and lowered the end of the barrel to aim just above the doorsill.

He shot when J.T. rolled on the ground in front of the open doorway. The slug tore into the top of J.T.'s head, sending blood flying into the wall across the street.

Hawk Nose hollered, "He got J.T.!"

Fargo heard Mad Jack yell back, "Don't just stand there, go get the bastard!"

"Naw, I ain't going in there alone," Hawk Nose complained. "Come gimme some help."

Fargo went to the door and peeked out to try to spot Hawk Nose, but he'd pulled back around the corner. Fargo whistled for the Ovaro. Within seconds he heard the pinto come around the corner and he whistled again. He holstered the Colt, braced himself on the doorjamb, then watched for the pinto to arrive. It did, trailed by the burro. He leapt into the saddle and had the rope free from the saddle horn before the stallion could wheel around and charge for the end of the street.

Rounding the corner, Fargo saw Hawk Nose cowering low against the wall. Fargo put two bullets in him, both in the head, reined the Ovaro, and shouted, "Chachona?"

She didn't answer. Four shots at him did. Mad Jack fired two while running crouched from the well to the mission. McCord escaped Fargo's shot by diving through the mission doorway. Marie then reappeared and shot twice while running zigzag as she retreated into the street leading to the corral. Fargo wasted a shot on her.

The Trailsman went for the nearest desperado. He had the Ovaro in a dead run when he came off the saddle just short of the front steps of the mission. On the ground, Fargo shot twice into the open doorway to intimidate Mad Jack and make him run for new cover. Pausing to reload, he heard Mad Jack McCord's fast-moving boot steps echo through the door. Fargo glanced to spot Marie, but she had opted to make tracks too.

Skye hugged the mission wall to the steps and up onto the landing. Taking a fresh breath, he grabbed the doorjamb and swung inside with the Colt up, its hammer cocked. McCord wasn't in sight. Fargo started down the aisle slowly. The sound of glass breaking somewhere in chambers behind the sanctuary temporarily halted Fargo's deadly search. He listened as he watched the two closed doors in the wall on either side of the altar. When he didn't hear any more sounds, he hurried to the door on the right.

Standing clear, he eased it open, removed his hat, and used it for bait. Just as he jerked it back, McCord shot twice, the bullets burying in the backrest of a front-row pew.

"Good try, McCord," Fargo taunted. "A mite slow, though."

When he heard a door open and close, Skye ducked to enter the room. Mad Jack had gone. Fargo hurried around a massive table in the center of the book-filled room to the only door.

Yanking it open, he chased after McCord, who was opening and closing doors behind him as he ran. Coming into the sanctuary, Fargo expected to see Mad Jack leaving through the front entrance. Instead, he heard muted footsteps above and off to the right. Half-turning, the Trailsman looked up. As he did, he saw a narrow opening in the side wall at the rear of the sanctuary.

Three long strides put him in it. He looked up a circular shaft with a stairway of flat stones and no handrails. The mission's big bell hung in the dome-shaped structure above the top of the shaft.

Fargo watched a shadow race over the inside of the dome and disappear. While easing up the stairway, he saw the bell rope jerk. The clapper rung the bell. Fargo rushed to the top and looked over the edge. McCord held on to the rope about ten feet below. The lifeless body of the priest still dangled from the end of the rope.

Grimacing, Fargo holstered the Colt, then grabbed the rope with both hands and started pulling. Slowly, the crown of McCord's hat came into view, then lowered from sight. McCord was going down about as quickly as Fargo heaved in rope.

Determined not to allow Mad Jack any slack, Fargo quickened the pace and increased the length of his heavings. The crown inched above the edge again. This time it did not lower. Another heave by Fargo and their eyes met.

Fargo paused to say grimly, "You have a choice, Jack. You can hang on with one hand and draw your gun with the other to try to shoot me, or you can climb back in and fight it out with me fist to fist. Remember this, though, while you make up your mind: the instant I see your gun, I'm releasing the rope."

He watched a nervous smile break across Mad Jack's face. Fargo pulled in one more length of the rope and said, "That's it, Jack. Now, let me see your hands come up and grab something solid."

First one, then the other hand came up and hooked over the adobe ledge. Fargo let go of the rope and massaged his hands as his adversary pressed over the ledge and rolled inside.

Fargo backed against the far ledge to give both himself and Mad Jack all the room possible. "Jack, I'm a fair man. You get thirty seconds to catch your breath and rub some feeling back in your hands. Then I'm going to kill you with my bare hands. I promise it will hurt a lot before you die."

Rubbing his hands, McCord said, "Look, it's the woman you want, not me. Let's make a deal. I'll throw in with you and—"

"Time's up," Fargo interrupted. He ducked under the bell and started around the shaft opening.

McCord glanced about nervously, threw up his hands, and shouted over his shoulder, "Mercier! Shoot this big son of a bitch!"

Fargo chuckled. "Come on, you sorry bastard, fight me. Don't have a woman do your dirty work. Hell, you might get lucky and beat me."

McCord put a leg over the banister, drew it back just as quickly, then started feigning left and right. Fargo countered his every move. Finally cornered, Mad Jack raised his fists. Fargo stared into his scared eyes and grinned. His powerful left fist struck with lightning speed into Mad Jack's jaw. McCord stumbled backward, grabbed the ledge with one hand to keep from toppling, and felt his sore jaw with the other.

Fargo watched the man's crossed eyes as he powered his right fist into his nose. It crunched loudly an instant before blood flew everywhere. "Please," Mad Jack groaned, "no more."

Fargo hit him hard in the gut. McCord's lungs emptied in a gush and he doubled over. Fargo brought his big right fist up in a powerful swing that knocked Mad Jack halfway over the ledge. Skye grabbed the man's bloody shirt and jerked him forward.

Nose to nose, Fargo snarled, "It's prayer time, Jack. You get five seconds."

"No," he grunted. "Please . . ."

Fargo grinned before giving Mad Jack a final kick in the chest and leaving him lying on the floor, unconscious.

Fargo stepped to the ledge and scanned along the structures and into the streets trying to spot Marie.

He saw a muzzle flash a split second before the bullet pinged off the bell. It came from a crack in the wall where he'd watched the sun rise and the night fall.

Fargo hurried down the stone steps, ran through the sanctuary, across the plaza, over the bridge, and up the stairway to the balcony. Moving slowly and cautiously, he went inside, checked the narrow hallway, then eased down the steps leading to his former place of confinement. The door stood wide open. He bent and looked in, saw nothing amiss, heard no sounds. With the Colt held before him, he stepped through the doorway. The space was empty. He glanced at the partly open side door, then hurried and looked outside. Three chickens were all he saw in the back alley.

After glancing left and right, he decided to head left. The alley led to another that crossed it. Again he chose left after noticing it connected with the street that led to the corral.

Halfway to the juncture, he heard a hammer cock behind him and he froze in midstride.

9

The husky female voice drawled, "You're a dead man, Fargo. Turn around real slow so I can see your handsome face and those pretty lake-blue eyes for the last time. You can look at me and think about what you could have had but didn't before I shoot you in the heart."

Fargo turned to see the black hole in the six-gun's barrel aimed at his heart. Marie stood there glaring at him. She wore the gun belt at her hips and she'd holstered the gun's twin.

Fargo anticipated her squeeze on the trigger and fell to his left. She fired. The slug buzzed less than an inch away from his right ear.

Before he could bring the Colt around to shoot, before she could squeeze off another round, a harsh Mexican voice shouted from behind him, "*Alto.*"

The Trailsman watched Marie move her gun hand and aim at the man, then pull the trigger. Fargo looked back in time to see two mounted *bandidos* at the end of the alleyway. One of them toppled to the ground. Fargo scooped up his Colt and shot the other man off the saddle. Wheeling to confront Marie, he saw she had disappeared.

The sound of several horses racing to the juncture where the two *bandidos* lay told Fargo that more trouble was on its way. He ran out of the tight alley to the livery where he'd been staked to the ground. He went to a crack in the front wall and peered out. Ten *bandidos* stood around the well watering their horses. All were looking to the right of him where the riders he heard had gone. Within seconds those riders would come through the wide back door. For him to flee up the stairs would mean trapping himself. Fargo sprinted through the wide door and ran right, away from the riders.

At the corner of the building he saw two narrow streets, one on his left, and the other began directly across from the building. He took the one on his left. He quickly found himself running in a maze of corridors that were wide enough for a horse but not for a wagon. He tried a few doors and found them secured. He heard the *bandidos* coming behind him, their loud shouts for people to open their doors, and guns firing off to his left.

As he continued running in the labyrinth, he wondered if the shooting meant they had cornered Marie. He took all the turns that led away from the gunfire. It seemed hopeless for him to find a way out of the confusing twists and abrupt turns of the narrow passages that formed Las Rocas. Twice he'd stopped and jumped to grab the lip of roofs and pull himself onto them, only to miss and fall to the ground. He quit trying when he heard the *bandidos* close behind.

Fargo rounded yet another corner and flattened his back to the wall to catch his breath and listen. Four different voices yelled to one another in the corridor he'd just left. He brought the Colt up and stepped back into the alleyway. The four men were running toward him. Fargo dropped two before the return fire moved him to turn and run.

Now that they had spotted him, he listened to them shout instructions to others giving chase. He knew it was only a matter of time before they boxed him in. He had to find his way back to the Ovaro so he could get the hell out of Las Rocas. They wanted Marie Mercier, not him, even though he was being doggedly pursued.

Rounding a corner at full speed, he collided with a person and both fell to the ground. He swung his Colt around to fire and pointed it into the muzzle of Marie's six-gun. She smiled and said, "Jesus, am I ever glad to see you."

"This is no time for making small talk. They're right behind me." He came to his feet and started running.

Marie followed in his bootsteps. "When this is over," she gasped, "I'll shoot it out with you. Right now we need each other."

"Like hell," he shot back. "The next alley we come to, you're going one way and I'm going the other."

Fargo went around a corner and halted abruptly. Marie plowed into his back. She was about to question him about why he'd stopped when she saw what faced them. They were in a short alley, a dead end. The adobe wall that surrounded Las Rocas was at the other end. Fargo raced to it. The top of the wall was too high for him to jump and climb over.

"What now?" Marie asked, gasping for breath.

"Get on my shoulders. I'll boost you up, then you can help me."

"Uh, huh, and what makes you think I will?"

"Honey, this fight isn't over. Like you said, you need me."

He squatted. She stood on his powerful shoulders. When he stood, she grabbed the top and swung a leg up on it. Marie had a perplexed expression on her face. Fargo said, "Well?"

She said, "I'm looking down the barrels of four guns, Mr. Fargo."

He turned to run. The entrance to the alley was filled with *bandidos* aiming their weapons at him. Several hammers were cocked above him. He glanced up and saw the men standing on the rooftops on either side of the passageway. Fargo dropped his Colt and stood, waiting for them to make the next move. One of the men on the roof told Marie to throw her guns over the wall, then come down with Fargo.

Under his breath, Fargo cursed the madman who designed the maze. The *bandidos* had no problem in finding their way out of it while marching Fargo and Marie to the *zócalo*.

They cut across one end of the plaza and entered the narrow dusty street that Fargo had taken earlier when going to the cantina. The bodies of Mullins and Neil littered the street.

The *bandidos* took Fargo and Marie to the door of the cantina and motioned them inside. The huge Mexican whom Fargo had seen leading the men during the fight at the stream stood behind the bar. Up close, the man looked mean and dangerous. Everything about him was big and rough-cut. He squinted though slitted eyelids at Marie. His big hands held a bottle of *tequila*. Chachona sat alone at a table, obviously frightened.

The big Mexican waved his men inside. They entered and spread out with their backs to the walls. Not including the women and himself, Fargo counted ten men. They appeared equally as dangerous as their leader, who grunted to Marie, "Come over here where I can see you better." He motioned for Fargo to stand by the door.

Marie went and stood across the bar from the huge man. He reached under the bar and came up with two bottles of *cerveza*. After pitching one to Fargo, he knocked the top off the other one and handed it to Marie. She refused it, staring icily into his eyes.

His eyebrows raised. "You don't like the way El Jefe opens bottles?"

"I don't drink beer," she replied, and reached for his *tequila*.

Letting her have it, he grunted, "Fine, *señorita*, drink whatever you like."

She took a swig and set the bottle in front of him. He picked it up, grabbed her by the hair, and pulled her head forward. He took a quick drink from the bottle before slapping Marie with a hard backhand that sent her reeling backward into a table. Wiping his face, he growled, "Where is the statue?"

She slumped in a chair and muttered, "I don't know."

"You lie," El Jefe bellowed. "The lady better tell me the truth or I'll make her wish she had. So, where did you hide it?"

"I don't know where it is," she repeated.

El Jefe snapped his fingers and ordered two of his men to bring her back to the bar. They yanked her from the chair and shoved her against the bar. Again El Jefe grabbed a fistful of her hair. He slapped her several times before asking if she had enough and was ready to tell him the truth. When he let go of her hair, she fell across the bartop and slid to the floor. El Jefe told two of his men to pick her up and lay her on the bar, while two other men brought more beer and liquor from the storage room for the rest. El Jefe tried to shake Marie awake. When she moaned but didn't open her eyes, he told one of the men to find some water.

Fargo watched a man run across the street and kick open the first door he came to. Within seconds he hurried back carrying a big water jug. He placed it on the bar and stood back.

El Jefe dipped a handful from it and splashed the water on her face. Two handfuls later, she sputtered and shook her head. El Jefe added another handful for good measure, then warned her, "Speak up, woman, or you'll wish you had. Where's that statue?"

When she didn't answer, he slapped her again. "You *will* talk!"

Marie groaned, "I don't know where it is."

El Jefe stood back, apparently to decide what to do next. Fargo watched him swill from a fresh bottle of *tequila*. With the bottle to his lips, he raised a foot and shoved Marie off the bar. She hit hard on the floor and didn't try to get up.

El Jefe took another drink, then hurled the bottle across the room. The big Mexican then came around the bar and jerked Marie to her feet.

Still groggy, she flailed wildly at him and spit in his face. His slap knocked her reeling into the men. El Jefe gestured for them to throw her back to him. Her chest slammed into his. She slumped to the floor. He pulled her up by the hair, slapped her face unmercifully, and shoved her away. Marie staggered and collapsed belly-down on Chachona's table.

El Jefe grunted as he moved back behind the bar. Staring at her, he got a fresh bottle.

Fargo looked at El Jefe and asked, "Okay if I stand outside while all this nonsense is going on?"

El Jefe told two of his men to stand across the street and guard Fargo, then waved him outside.

Fargo drew small circles in the dirt while listening to the hollers coming from the storeroom.

Finally, El Jefe appeared in the doorway with a beer bottle in one hand and a bottle of tequila in the other. Handing the beer down to Fargo, he said, "It looks like we could be here for a while. She's not giving up easily."

After a swallow of the warm beer, Fargo told him, "I don't think you will get anything out of her this way. The woman is very tough. My guess is she can take whatever you give her."

El Jefe grunted and went back inside.

Chachona appeared in the doorway. In a low voice she said, "If I was her, I would tell."

"Marie won't tell," Fargo predicted. "She would die before telling."

"Maybe she is telling the truth. What do you think?"

While he felt sure Marie knew exactly where it was, he kept the thought to himself and suggested, "He will never find it if he kills her. And there's no way his men can make her talk. They can really hurt her, yes. But make her talk? No, Chachona, this isn't the way to make her tell."

Chachona eased back inside the cantina.

When Fargo heard El Jefe's palm slam on the top of the bar, he stood and went inside. El Jefe snarled, "I'm getting tired of nothing happening."

To Marie, El Jefe said, "I think the *señorita* better tell where the statue is. *Sí*, Chachona?"

Chachona gulped first. In a low voice she answered, "*Sí*, Jefe." Looking at Marie, she suggested, "Tell him. It will be easier that way."

By now, Fargo had all of it he could take. He went to the bar and said, "There's an easier way. Do you want to hear it?"

"I will make her tell."

"Maybe, but I don't think so."

"Then tell me your way."

"I think she is a narcissist. *Comprende*?"

El Jefe stared at the ceiling for a moment before admitting, "No, *señor*. What is this narsisst?"

"Marie Mercier adores her image, especially her beautiful face."

El Jefe's eyes widened. He was quick to grasp Fargo's meaning. "Feo, you and Chato bring Marie to me."

Feo approached. An ugly scar began just below his hairline, coursed down his forehead, split the left eyebrow, and ended on his stubbled chin.

"*Señorita*, you have convinced me that beating you won't make you tell me the truth." He drew his long knife and held the cutting edge in front of her eyes.

116

"You see that ugly scar on Feo's face." He looked at Feo. "Step over here, Feo, and let her see your face."

Feo came and looked down at her. "Ugly, wouldn't you say, *señorita*?"

"Yes," Marie whispered. Her eyes widened and the perpetually upturned corners of her lips disappeared.

El Jefe motioned Feo closer, saying, "Look out the door so the light will be on your face." Glancing from the scar to Marie's face, he positioned the tip of the knife blade to touch her hairline.

"No," Marie cried. "Please don't cut me!"

The tip remained in place. "One last time. Where is it?"

"The statue isn't in Las Rocas. One of my men left with it last night."

Nodding, El Jefe answered, "Where did he take it?"

Fargo cocked an ear to hear the reply better. "Guaymos," she said.

El Jefe took the tip away. His eyes darting left to right below his furrowed brow conveyed his puzzlement. "Did you say Guaymos? Why Guaymos?"

"A French schooner is docked there. We were on our way to Guaymos to hand it over to the captain when things got out of hand." She glanced at Fargo.

El Jefe looked at him and said, "Is she lying?"

During Fargo's pause to find the right words, Chachona answered, "Most everybody in Las Rocas says they saw something big carried in here. They couldn't see what because it was covered with a *sarape*."

Almost instantly one of the *bandidos* held up the serape Fargo had seen in the storage room. The fellow nodded toward the rear of the barroom and said, "I found this *sarape* in the back room when I went to get the beer." He tossed it to El Jefe.

He caught it, grunted, and glanced at Chachona. "What about this *sarape, señorita*?"

"I don't know, *señor*. I never saw it before now," Chachona replied.

His gaze moved on to Fargo. "What about it, *amigo*? Is the woman lying?"

"I don't think so," he replied. "Marie had her men stake me to the ground in that building on the other side of the stream, across from the plaza and mission. There are a few cracks in the wall. During the night I heard somebody walk across the bridge, then I got a fleeting look at him when he headed toward the corral. It happened so fast that I couldn't make out who it was. After a little while the person came back, this time on a horse trailing a donkey. The donkey had been rigged to pack. The rider crossed between the well and mission. I presume he came here."

Fargo saw Marie relax, and she began to breathe easier.

El Jefe grunted, pulled on an earlobe, and inquired, "Who killed the Texicans that we found here?"

"I did," Fargo answered. "After shooting them, I searched the place and spotted the serape in the back room. When I removed it, I saw a section cut from a tree trunk, not the statue I expected. So, I put two and two together and assumed the rider had taken it. That's why I say she might not be lying to you."

El Jefe ordered Chato to check the back room for a tree trunk. While he was gone, El Jefe asked Fargo, "Why did you come to Las Rocas?"

"Same reason as you. To get the statuette of Our Lady. Only I intended to return her to Domingo."

Chato came back with the hunk of wood. El Jefe nodded, withdrew a bottle of tequila from under the bar, and stared at the ceiling, apparently searching for answers or a decision, while pulling out the cork. After taking a slug of the tequila, he belched, then scanned the expressionless faces of his men and said, "Everybody who believes he heard the truth go outside." When none moved, El Jefe stabbed the sharp point of the knife into the top of the counter.

They all headed for the doorway. The last man to leave paused and changed his mind. "No, Jefe, I say the woman lied. I think it's still here in Las Rocas, and she and the big man know where."

El Jefe grunted. "What makes you think so, Lobo Loco? Eh? What did you see or hear that we did not?"

Fargo studied the wild-eyed man, noting the cruel set of his jaw, thin lips partly hidden by his bushy mustache. In a way, the man looked as dangerous as his name, Crazy Wolf, implied.

"Anglos are masters of lies and deceit. I've been to El Paso, so I know. If we believe her and ride for Guay—"

El Jefe slammed a fist onto the bar to interrupt Lobo Loco. "No," the leader bellowed. "Too many of my men say they heard the truth. I agree with them. This time you are wrong, Lobo. We ride for Guaymos."

"*Sí*, Jefe. I go where you lead."

El Jefe came from behind the bar, strode victoriously outside, and stuck a foot in the stirrup of his waiting mount. Swinging up in the saddle, he looked at Fargo and said, "*Hasta luego, amigo.*" To the others he shouted, "To Guaymos! *Vamos!*"

As Lobo Loco left through the doorway, Fargo heard him mumble, "It isn't there."

10

Fargo went behind the bar and got three beers. As he pulled the corks, he looked at the two women and wondered why El Jefe had left Marie behind. "Had it been me, I would have taken you along," he told her dryly. Marie's eyebrows raised slightly and she shrugged, as though to say she agreed. He set one of the bottles on the bar in front of her and handed one to Chachona as he passed her on his way to the door. He looked down the street filled with dust raised by the departing *bandidos* and watched the stragglers disappear around the corner at the plaza. "Hell, I believe I would have taken all three of us," he muttered. Fargo tipped his bottle and swigged from it.

Chachona stood looking out the broken window. "What now, Fargo?" she asked.

Walking back behind the bar, he answered, "Hard to tell." His gaze focused on Marie's haggard face.

"Quit staring at me," she snapped.

"You look like hell," he told her.

"Yes, well, I feel like I've just crawled up out of hell. I'll live."

Staring out into the street, Chachona remarked, "You didn't have to go through that beating and all." She broke the stare and glanced over her shoulder at Marie to add, "Why didn't you tell him when he first asked? That would have been the end of it."

Marie answered cuttingly without turning to her.

"Don't look at me with that phony pity in your eyes. I knew what I was doing. What I don't understand is"—she spun her back to the counter and eyed Chachona—"how do you fit into all of this? How come they left you alone?" She turned and rested her elbows on the bar.

It was a good question, one that Fargo wondered about. But he kept quiet and waited to hear Chachona's response.

Chachona's eyes blazed as she half-turned to face Marie. "What makes you think it didn't happen?"

Fargo wondered about that too. It was possible. She may not have escaped through a back window like she said. He tried to recall if he'd seen any back windows in the mission and couldn't. He took a sip of the tepid *cerveza* and watched the two women. Both were spoiling for a fight.

Though she was shorter than Marie by at least six inches and easily fifteen pounds lighter, Chachona's eyes nevertheless flashed anger as she left the window and came toward the tall brunette.

Fargo grimaced. Chachona pounced, raking her fingernails down Marie's already badly scraped back. Marie shrieked, whirled around, and backhanded her. Chachona stumbled sideways, caught her balance, and lunged with clawed hands aimed to tear into Marie's face.

"I wanted to kill you the first time I saw you," Chachona yelled. "I don't know why El Jefe let you live!"

Fargo sensed that the two women were prepared to fight it out—something he neither had the time nor the patience to watch.

After a studious moment, he said, "Both of you keep quiet and come over to the bar." He stepped in front of them and said sternly, "We still have plenty of work to do. If you two want to fight, do it later, when

I'm not around." Fargo then spun on his heels and headed for the door.

Without looking back, he stepped through the doorway and headed for the plaza. En route he went back and forth across the street to knock hard on doors and shout, "Come out! It's safe!"

Chachona then Marie staggered out onto the street and threaded their way through people curious and brave enough to believe Fargo's words and come outside. Fargo heard a female voice ask, "*Qué pasó?*"

Chachona answered, "What happened was, this whore and her gang of thieves stole a statue of Our Lady of Guadalupe from the mission at Domingo and brought it here. Then it disappeared. The *bandidos* came for it. You are safe now because they have left and all the Anglo men are dead."

At the corner Fargo noticed his weapons and Marie's lying on the ground next to the wall on his right. He squatted and loaded his Colt, then rose with everything else in his hands.

He loaded the Sharps while ambling across the square, then he headed for the bridge to the two-story building. Chachona appeared at his side, then Marie as she caught up with them.

Marie asked, "What do you plan to do, Fargo?"

"Check your room for weapons, then eat some real food."

Chachona heard him, then glanced about to single out one of the local women. Waving to the woman, Chachona shouting, "Over here, *señora*! I have something for you to do!"

The woman angled toward them and approached as they neared the bridge. "*Sí?*" she asked in a tiny voice.

Crossing behind Marie and Fargo, Chachona cited her menu to the woman. "Make tortillas for three. Cook lots of eggs. Make rice and beans. Plenty of both. Cook two chickens. The best you have. Salsa too. Prepare a table for us on the balcony. We also want some milk to drink while we eat. *Comprende?*"

"*Sí, señorita*," the chubby woman replied.

Chachona dismissed her with a wave of the hand, and the woman hurried on her way.

Fargo led them onto the balcony and down the narrow hallway to the only door he hadn't tried earlier. Kicking it open, he went inside. The coiled bullwhip lay on a chair. He snaked an arm into the coil and worked the bullwhip up to ride on his left shoulder. Marie's change of clothes lay in a heap on the floor at the foot of an unmade bed. He nudged the clothing with a toe to check for a knife or gun. He decided the room was clean of weaponry.

Waving the two women inside, he told Marie, "Okay, you can get your stuff."

"Uh, huh," she began as she went to her clothing. "I would have thought you wanted me to undress."

He said nothing while watching her step to a bureau and open the top drawer. Fargo warned, "Whoa, Marie. Don't reach in."

He came up beside her and looked in the drawer. The only things inside were the bracelet, necklace, and the silver waist chain. He put them in his pocket. When she began to complain, he told her, "Later, perhaps."

Chachona waited for Marie to leave the room and fell in behind her. Fargo followed them to the balcony. As Chachona had ordered, two young females were setting a table. They stood back when the two older women approached. Marie and Chachona sat to face each other, leaving the seat that overlooked the *zócalo* for Skye Fargo.

He sat and drank his glass of fresh milk, then handed the empty glass to one of the waiting teenage females. Looking at the mission, he said, "After siesta, Marie and I head back to Domingo. What about you, Chachona?"

"Chachona?" Marie cried. "She can go to hell. Don't I have any say in this?"

"No," Fargo replied easily, "you don't. Honey, you're the problem, not her."

"So? Leave me here and your problem is over."

"No, Marie, you have to answer for what you have done. You're going to Domingo with me. Again, Chachona, do you want to ride with us?"

Before she could answer, Marie yelled, "Go ahead and shoot me, you big son of a bitch! Shoot me here and now and get it done and over. I'm not going back to Domingo. Not with you, not with anyone else."

"I don't shoot women," he began slowly, an edge of warning in the tone, "unless they're pointing a gun at me or—"

The arrival of the hefty woman and two slim helpers, all bearing platters of food, interrupted him and left his sentence hanging. For a few moments the steam rising from the food-laden platters flooded the immediate area with the succulent aroma of zesty Mexican food.

"Shut up and eat," Fargo ordered. He raked a helping of eggs into his plate and chased them with some of the refried beans and rice. While he devoured his meal, the two women picked at theirs.

Wiping his mouth with a cloth napkin, he glanced at Chachona and asked, "Well?"

Chachona put her fork in her plate. "*Sí.* I'm not needed here. Not at this time, anyhow."

"Good," he replied. "In that case I have a job for you." Cutting his eyes to Marie, he explained, "You can watch her while I take a nap." He handed Chachona his Sharps.

They watched him stand and go down the stairway and walk to the well. He elbowed his way through the women waiting their turn to fill their water jugs and went to the front. As Chachona watched him dump a bucketful of water on his head and shoulders, she hissed, "I hope you start trouble."

Marie smiled. "I will. You can count on it." After a pause, she added, "When he least expects it."

Fargo's eyes snapped open. He stared at the paint-flaked ceiling for a moment, then let his gaze drift to the window. From the way the light spilled through it, creating an ill-defined, barely perceptible pattern on the wood floor, he reckoned the hour was near four o'clock.

He sat on the edge of the bed momentarily to yawn and scratch his back, then stood and went to the window. He looked out over the long narrow rows of dwellings separated by even more narrow streets that created the semilabyrinth of the village.

Far in the northeast, almost on the flat horizon, the rock formation stood like a sentinel, its western surfaces glistening under the lowering sun.

He glanced to the cloudless, soft-azure sky before retreating to the bed and sitting on its edge to pull on his clothes. He stuck Marie's two guns in his waistband. Walking out into the hall, he swung his gun belt around his hips and fastened the buckle. On the balcony, he saw the table had been cleared of food and dishes.

He went to the railing and looked down on the square. A lone woman was hauling up the water bucket. He noted the hanged priest had been taken down and his body, and those of the *federales*, had been taken away. The bell rope hung straight down from the lever above the bell. All was quiet.

Returning to the hallway, Fargo found Marie and Chachona in the third room he checked. Chachona sat on the floor in a corner, the Sharps in her hand. Her right index finger rested on the trigger guard and her head was against one of the walls. She was sound asleep, breathing slow and easy.

Marie had woken up when Fargo entered the room, and now she sat up on the bed, eyeing Fargo as he went over to Chachona and nudged her with his foot. She awakened with a start. Before he could stop her, she raised the Sharps and pulled the trigger. A chunk of adobe splintered out of the wall.

Now that she saw it was him, she came to her feet and peered around him to make sure Marie hadn't escaped. "You scared me," she said weakly.

"Good shot," he told her through a grin.

Embarrassed, Chachona stood up and began gathering her things.

Fargo led the women to the plaza. He whistled for the Ovaro and told Chachona to go find her mount, he would take Marie to the corral so she could saddle up.

At the corral, he watched while Marie made the mare ready to ride. As she laid on the saddlebags, Chachona rode up. Fargo waved her inside the corral, then bent through the rails and fetched a coiled rope looped over a fence post. He secured one end to the mare's bridle and the other to Chachona's saddle horn. He warned her to watch for slack in the trailing rope, in case Marie got fancy ideas about riding up to snatch the Sharps from her. That done, he got on the pinto and told them to come on. Minutes later they passed through the north gap in the adobe wall. Fargo angled northeast.

They rode in silence until twilight. Fargo stopped them a long stone's throw from the formation of rocks, saying, "We'll rest and cook something to eat, catch a few winks of sleep, and be on our way." He dismounted and went to look for some firewood.

When he came back, he found the women sitting about ten feet apart with Chachona aiming the Sharps at Marie's head. He dropped the wood on the ground between them and said, "Chachona, build us a small fire and cook something to eat. You'll find some grub in my saddlebags. I'll watch her."

Chachona started the fire, while Marie watched Fargo unsaddle all three horses. He brought their bedrolls close to Chachona.

He told Marie, "Honey, you may not like doing it, but I think it's best if you come out of those clothes." When she smiled and quickly began to comply, he explained, "No, I don't want your body. I just don't want you to run off while I'm asleep. Naked, the sun would burn you to death before high noon.

"And, ma'am, don't even think about getting to a gun to shoot us. Before I lie down and close my eyes, you'll be tied to the Ovaro.

"Don't think you can lead the stallion to me, either. Try and you'll discover he raises hell no matter how gentle you are with him. That horse knows when to come to me and when not to. But you're free to try."

Still holding the smile, Marie stood to pull off her riding skirt. Sitting again, she drew her knees up to her waist. Fargo shook his head.

"I want my jewelry," Marie said. "May I?"

He pulled all three pieces from his pocket and pitched them to her.

As Marie fastened the waist chain, Chachona asked, "What's that for?"

Without glancing up, Marie told her, "Makes me feel good, makes me sexy. Eh, Fargo?"

He grunted and kept his thoughts about it to himself. He watched her bring the compact out and look in the mirror to check around her eyes.

They gazed at the moon while they ate beans and munched on beef jerky.

Fargo inched back to his bedroll and spread it open. Marie watched him take hers about twenty paces toward the rock formation and unroll it. He wiggled a finger for Marie to get on it. When she did, he used the trailing rope to lash her wrists together behind her and tied the other end to the Ovaro. "Sweet dreams, ma'am," he told her, and walked back to his bedroll.

Chachona sat and watched him undress for bed. As he lay down, her eyes darted from his length to Marie, who had already fallen asleep.

She put her tin plate aside and released the draw-string holding her dress at her shoulders. Sliding the garment down her body, she rose and stepped out of it, glanced at Marie, then approached him. The after-glow from the dwindling fire accentuated her shapely curves and cast her heavy breasts in dark erotic shadows. He watched her eyes as she knelt at his waist and fondled his manhood.

Stroking it, she bent over him and pressed her open mouth to his. As her hot tongue darted about inside his mouth and caressed his tongue, she pulled on his length till it swelled with blood. When it was hard and erect, fully extended, she broke the wet kiss and moaned.

He pulled her higher up on him and fed as much of her right breast between his lips and into his mouth as it would hold. Then he smothered the smooth mound with his tongue, not overlooking the hard nipple it found, nor the small circle from which it proudly pro-truded. She moaned with delight and mewed, "Oh, that is so good, *señor*, so good. Please, oh, please, don't stop. Do the other one too."

His tongue slid over, teased the nipple, then he took in a mouthful of the velvety breast. He rocked his head from side to side, and his hand stole down over her quivering abdomen, paused to rub on her thick patch of pubic hair, then continued to her tender loins. She parted her legs for him and he slipped the middle finger between the moist, hot lips. She immediately began a series of quick gasps and squirmed her hips to urge the long finger to probe inside. When it did, she trembled, moaning, "Take me, take me, *señor*."

Fargo rolled her beneath him, then dragged his member across her soft belly. As he continued bringing his hot, throbbing member up, she clamped it between her breasts and massaged it vigorously before releasing him to probe in her open, eagerly awaiting mouth.

As the crest slipped through her wet lips, she moaned loudly and brought her head up to gorge her mouth and upper throat with as much of him as both could take. Her begging tongue went to work, exploring, slithering over the crest, slipping back down the underside, teasing around that inside and outside her tight lips, then retreating to suckle furiously.

Fargo slowly pulled away from Chachona. Her lips smacked when the crown popped free. Breathing rapidly and hard, she gasped, "Santa María, that was so good. I want more. Give it to me. All of it."

He settled down between her thighs, which needed no coaxing from him to open wide. Raising her knees and hips to accommodate him better, she whimpered, "Fill me now."

He probed the head between the slippery lips, which had swollen in anticipation of this moment. During the brief parting of them, her legs wrapped around his waist and she locked her ankles on his hard butt and pressed them tightly to it, as though he might try to escape. Then she pushed upward when he shoved down. Most all of his member powered down the soft but tight tunnel.

Chachona screamed, "Aaaaagh . . . aaaaagh! Eeee-yaaiii!"

Their hips gyrated in opposite directions, with her meeting his comebacks and thrusts with her own to milk the most out of the moonlit encounter as she could, sacrificing endurance for unmitigated lightning-fast pleasure. That she had entered a state of ecstasy came in her joyous shrieks. "Deeper, Fargo!"

He felt her ankles dig on his butt to help him succeed. "Eeeeyaaiii," she shrieked. Fargo's hips drove downward as hard as he could move them, fusing the base to her widely parted lower lips at the end of each long plunge.

Chachona's fingernails dug into his muscled back at the shoulders and she begged for him to go faster. "*Más rápido,*" she squealed. "Please . . . aaaaghh . . . aaaaghh!"

He felt her tight contraction begin, and hurried to climax with her orgasm. She signaled it coming when the fingernails ripped up across his shoulders and she screamed, "Aaaagh!" She was in a frenzy now, dragging her lips and tongue over his chest and raking his waist with her knees. She locked and opened her legs, pressing her feet on the bedroll to keep him from slipping out of her slickened nook, and gasping hard.

When she bit into his left pectoral muscle, he probed deeply and held it there while erupting a steady flow, then withdrew by an inch or so when the spurts started.

She lowered her legs reluctantly. In quick panting breaths, she sighed, "I'm so happy. That was *excelente, señor.*" When he rolled off her and laid on his back, she eased onto him and kissed him gratefully, then lingered to nibble his lips, cheeks, and on each ear.

After catching his wind, he urged her off him and sat up. He glimpsed a sparkle in the rock formation well behind Marie's sleeping form. He glanced up at the bright moon, now realizing a moonbeam had kissed off something other than the smooth surface of one of the vertical, monolithic stones. Fixing his vision on the area from which the gleam came, he pulled on his Levi's, rose, and started walking straight toward the spot.

Marie woke as Fargo walked past her. She rose onto

her knees and stretched a hand to grab him, but he swerved away and continued on.

Approaching the stones, he angled left and kept his gaze focused on where he'd seen the sparkle. Coming closer, he stopped, tilted his head back, and leaned from side to side in hope he would see the gleam and get a positive fix on it. No amount of head tilting or moving about produced the glimmer again. Knowing his eyes hadn't played a trick on him, he went around the stones to see what the moonbeam had struck.

Looking up, he stumbled and nearly fell over something. In the shadows lay the donkey, still rigged for packing, and clearly dead.

Fargo dropped to his knees and searched over the sand with the palms of his hands to find boot prints and learn where they led.

He soon found them, and he felt his way to a small opening in the base of the formation. He crawled through it, waited for his vision to adjust, and saw he was in a natural tunnel. The irregular, often coarse surfaces of the winding tunnel made passage difficult. While crawling through it, he collected a few scrapes to go along with those carved in his hide by Chachona.

Twisting around a jagged curve in the tight shaft, the darkness gave way to soft moonlight. He paused and looked through the inner mouth of the rock conduit and into the eyes of the largest rattlesnake he'd ever seen.

The huge diamondback was coiled, poised to strike. It occupied every inch of the ground where the inner surfaces of the tall stones met and formed a small sandy area. Sweat rolled down Fargo's chiseled face as he watched the deadly reptile's unblinking eyes and flicking slender tongue. Its long wide rattler jiggled, came up, and started signaling the serpent's imminent intention to paralyze the intruder.

The curving, twisting wall behind him was too close

to allow a fast back-away. Neither could he move forward, not even by an inch. The slightest movement would trigger the strike. But he knew he had to move before the diamondback did. While he got prepared, he hoped the snake would hesitate a moment longer.

Ever so slowly he dug his fingers into the soft layer of sand until they were deep enough so that when he closed them his hands would be full. The snake's big, heart-shaped head stayed rock-steady, its eyes fixed on the target.

A cloud of sand flew from beneath Fargo and showered the rattler's head. Blinded, it struck. Fargo dodged left. His big right hand grabbed around the slim part of the snake's otherwise fat length behind its head. Fargo yanked the head back.

For an instant Fargo and the rattler were eye-to-eye: he with gritted teeth and staring at the puffy white venom sac and the membrane covering the inside of huge open mouth; it spewing venom from the two needle-sharp fangs. As the snake's long, thick, and heavy length swept forward and curled around his arm, Fargo shoved its open mouth and head down in the sand, held it there, and inched his way through the opening.

Outside, he stood in the tiny space and held the still-dangerous head away from him as far as possible. With the other hand he pulled its body free from its curled grip on him. He drove the ugly head into the sharp edges on the monolith's inner surfaces until the head was a bloody mess. Fargo flung the serpent into the tunnel opening to die.

Now he considered his surroundings. The surfaces of the stones angled out as they rose skyward. Unlike the windblown smooth outer surfaces, these inner ones were jagged, in places almost stairlike. He believed that climbing up would present no problem for a sure-footed person such as himself.

Fargo started the ascent of Las Rocas, moving steadily toward the area where he believed he'd find the source of the glint. He came to it near the summit, wedged between two of the monoliths and standing on a tilted rock ledge connecting them.

Our Lady stood facing out through the narrow slot, as though offering grace and peace to passersby.

He grasped the statuette and lifted it to test its weight. It was lighter than he expected. Father Bonelli, he recalled, had said thirty, maybe thirty-five pounds. She weighs less than that, Fargo thought. The good *padre* quite obviously never handled a fifty-pound bag of beans. Getting a new hold on it, the Trailsman found why it didn't weight more than it did, as much as its size would make a person think: the inside had been hollowed to leave a shell about an inch thick.

Taking a firm grip on her bejeweled crown, he lowered the statuette beside him and began descending slowly to the stand space. The rattlesnake posed a problem. While it lay more or less where and how he left it, that didn't mean it was yet completely lifeless. Fargo knew it was possible for a near-dead rattler, especially one of this size, to inject a lethal dose of its venom if it felt one of its fangs touch something. He would have to avoid the head, which he couldn't see.

He clutched the figurine to his chest, backed into the opening, and lowered himself to lie on his back with his head toward the far entrance. The diamondback lay alongside the base of the dome-shaped passageway on his right. Using his feet and left hand for leverage, he inched forward until his shoulder brushed against the snake's body. The body trembled.

Pausing, he strained to see where the head was, and how close. He couldn't tell. "We can't lay here all night," he mumbled.

After crowding against the left wall, he balanced Our Lady on his torso and reached his right hand until he touched the snake's body. He started pulling it back toward the inner opening, hoping the head would follow in a straight line. He watched the dim form creep past less than an inch from his eyes.

When the head came alongside his, he ceased pulling back on the body and stared at the long fangs that extended from the pulpy glob that had once been a mighty head. Venom dripped from both fangs. He couldn't risk one of them catching in his hide when he squirmed forward. He reached up and broke a thin sliver of rock from the dome. He used the sliver to milk the sacs dry of venom, then continued inching his way through the shaft and outside.

He carried the figurine out into the bright moonlight and stood it on the sand to have a look.

"You're a beauty, all right," he told Our Lady. "Tight-lipped too, and with clothes nobody can take off. Richer than all of Saint Louis and can't spend a penny of it."

He walked around the figurine to look it over. A diamond-encrusted crown encircled the hood of her cape; the roses on the cape had been fashioned exquisitely out of inlaid bright-red rubies; and the edges of the cape were trimmed with sapphires, jade, different shades of red rubies, tiny diamonds, pearls, and strands of silver thread.

The black crescent on which she stood was of highly polished black onyx. The myriad of pointed spires that emanated from the sides and surrounded the figurine symbolized her halo.

Fargo marveled at the design. Whoever did it, he thought, had a good imagination and plenty of gold and silver.

Each spire composing the halo was made of five thin pieces of precious metals. The main middle piece was shaped from a thin plate of gold. On either side of it were slightly smaller spires made of silver. On them were even smaller spires fashioned from gold.

The designs that covered her long gown had been done with threads of gold and silver, while the design for the collar was carved from ivory.

He took Our Lady in his arms and headed back to camp.

Halfway there, the women rushed to meet him. He had to grin when Marie hit the end of her rope and the elasticity of it snapped her off her feet and flipped her head over heels back toward the immovable pinto.

Chachona ran up to him and dropped to her knees. Above her gaping mouth, widened eyes stared awestruck at Our Lady's head bowed in prayer. Chachona's right hand raised slowly, as though she was in a trance, and she crossed herself just as slowly. She looked up at Fargo and smiled and sighed.

He stepped around her and headed for the soft glow of the embers left by the cooking fire. Chachona sprinted past him to add twigs to the embers. She was blowing on the coals when Fargo arrived and stood the statue in a place several feet from the new flames, where they all could view it.

As the flames spread and licked higher, a burst of color adorned Our Lady. The diamonds glittered. The highly polished rubies mirrored the flickering flames in tiny miniatures. The other precious stones and the spires constituting her halo, all shimmered and glowed. It was as though Our Lady had come to life and stood in a shaft of heavenly light.

Marie said, "It's mine."

Chachona shot back, "No, she's mi—!"

But Fargo's quick reply to Marie's statement cut Chachona's claim short. "You can look, but you can't touch."

"Before this is over, I'll have it," Marie snapped.

Fargo went to his saddle and retrieved the bullwhip. Walking toward Marie, he uncoiled it and let it pay out behind him. When he halted well in front of her, she stood and struck a defiant pose with legs apart, spine ramrod-erect and broad shoulders straight. "Damn you," she snarled.

He snapped the whip a few times for warm-up and to get the feel of this particular whip. While doing it, he remarked rather dryly, "Been a long time since I had a whip in my hands. Can't recall if I held it with the left or right. All I remember is leaving that she-bear in bloody shreds." He changed hands and popped the tip clumsily a few times. "Yeah, this is the hand," he muttered loud enough for her to hear.

Flipping the tip into position behind him, he continued, "Honey, I don't want to hear another word from you the rest of this trip."

"Give that whip to me," Chachona cried. "I'll give her more. I'll whip her big butt off."

"No," Fargo sighed, "she's had enough for now." Coming back to the saddle, he coiled the bullwhip.

Marie shouted, "No guts, Fargo! You had me and walked away. No guts. Were you holding back because I'm female? That it, big man?" Now she taunted him. "I'm not afraid of you. Give me a chance and I'll show you how big a coward you really are."

For a few seconds he looked at her, then went and let her loose. She swung a fist at his face, but he caught her wrist. Grinning, he said, "Marie, we're going to fight fairly, just the way you've always wanted to do it."

He shoved her before him and took her to the saddles and tack, where her gun belt and six-guns were. She and Chachona watched him put one bullet in one of her guns and move the chambered round into position to fire. Handing the gun belt to her, he said, "Strap it on, Marie, it's show time in the desert."

She whipped it around her waist and buckled it to ride on her hips. As she did, Fargo strapped on his gun belt. He let them see him take out all the cartridges in the Colt and put one back in. He spun the cylinder without watching where the bullet stopped.

"That fair enough for you?" he asked. "I'll tie my gun hand behind me and draw from across if you want."

Chachona recognized a bad situation when she saw one. She squalled, "*Señor, está usted loco*? The woman will kill you—and me!"

"That's right," Marie replied through a devilish smile. "I'll put the bullet between those pretty lake-blue eyes. I'll leave both of you for the buzzards."

"One hitch," Fargo answered.

"What's that?" Marie asked, squinting.

"We do it fair and square. Ten paces, turn and fire. I promise it will be your last walk."

Marie laughed.

Fargo glanced at Chachona sitting next to the figurine. "When I say start, you count to ten real slow."

He looked up at the moon, then led Marie to a position where the moonlight wouldn't favor either of them. Dropping her gun in its holster, he winked at her and said, "This is it, honey. Turn around and put your back to mine."

"She'll cheat," Chachona warned.

"No, I won't," Marie shot back.

Fargo told Chachona to start counting.

They parted when she began counting, "*Uno . . . dos . . . tres . . . cuatro . . . cinco . . .*"

A coyote howled mournfully on the count of *seis*, then a glistening stick in front of him began to coil on *siete*. Its rattle started to buzz on *ocho*.

Fargo hesitated in midstride, whipped out the Colt, and threw down on the rattler's head. The hammer snapped on empty chambers twice before the Colt fired and the bullet tore the snake's head off. The explosion had been so loud that for an instant Fargo expected to see the Colt falling apart in his hand. Then he realized another shot had been fired at the same time.

He spun in time to see Marie sink to the ground where she had stopped to turn on him two paces short of ten. Blood gushed from her chest where the Sharps bullet had pierced her heart.

When she slumped forward, Chachona quickly completed the count. He turned to congratulate her for protecting his backside, but before he could speak, she swung the Sharps to aim at his heart.

Sighting down the rock-steady barrel, she began her confession, "*Sí, señor*, I am one of El Jefe's people. The Texicans came and stole Our Lady before El Jefe was to arrive. After I saw you, then her leave Domingo, the priest told us you were going to get Our Lady and bring her back. I rode and told El Jefe what had happened.

"He sent me to Las Rocas to be his spy and learn where they had the statue. El Jefe didn't know if the woman told the truth or lied. So he stabbed his knife on the bar. That told us not to kill the woman or you. I was to stay close to you because you would keep her with you. That way, if she lied, you would learn the truth and lead me to the statue. El Jefe isn't stupid."

As she spoke, Fargo saw a Gila monster come from behind Our Lady and move out of sight behind Chachona's rump nestled in the sand. It was time for him to buy a little more time while the reptile made up its mind, for it didn't reappear from behind her. He said, "What did El Jefe want you to do if we went back to Domingo without the statue?"

She began answering, "I was to ki—" Chachona's eyes grew large. She screamed, dropped the Sharps, and grabbed for her ass. She screamed again, louder than before, brought her hands around, and tried to shake the Gila monster free of its mouth's grip on the side of her left hand. When she couldn't, the terrified woman sprung to her feet and started running toward the rocks, screaming and pulling on the reptile.

He watched her stumble, fall, try to get up, then make it to her knees and continue screaming.

Fargo looked at Our Lady's peaceful face before he picked up the Sharps, aimed, and put Chachona out of her misery.

To sleep now would be next to impossible. After pulling on the rest of his clothes and rolling the bedroll, he saddled Marie's mare and secured Our Lady on top of it, along with Marie's saddlebags. He felt something odd on the underside of the saddlebags. He took them to the fire for a closer inspection. Picking along a seam where one shouldn't have been, it parted. Odd, he thought. It's a damn flap of some kind.

He found it easy to pull open. Money covered the inside of the shallow compartment. He sat and counted five thousand dollars. He whistled softly under his breath and glanced to Marie. The pinto walked up. Fargo transferred the money to his saddlebags and made the Ovaro ready to ride with the mare trailing.

He looked at the statuette and slowly shifted his gaze to Marie. Fargo dismounted and went to her clothes to get the silver compact. Walking back to the stallion, he put it in his pocket.

As Fargo rode away from the death site, the coyote howled anew. He glanced to his right and saw the coyote sitting on top of one of Las Rocas.

11

Since shortly after nightfall Fargo had the uneasy feeling that somebody was following him. He'd looked over his shoulder several times, even reined to a halt once when the moon was low on the horizon to turn and listen while peering into the nearly ink-black night. He neither heard nor saw anything out of the ordinary.

A little past midnight, he arrived on the outskirts of Domingo. Moments later, the Ovaro and mare passed through the entrance in the south wall. The streets were deserted at this hour. Domingo was asleep. The only sounds were made by the horse's soft hooffalls and his saddle when he moved on it.

Passing by the cantina, he saw the door was closed. No light escaped through its edges to betray the presence of anyone inside. Lupita's door was also closed. He shook his head, wondered why these people slept behind closed doors and windows during the hot nights.

He stopped at the well to water the horses. After quenching their thirst, and his, he walked them to the front steps of the mission. There he removed the statuette and stood it on the ground. He released the mare, coiled his rope, and hung it on his saddle. As he did, he glanced up sharply, almost expecting to see someone coming across the square. The uneasy feeling of being observed was still with him. There was no one on the *zócalo*, nor anywhere else that he could see.

He patted the Ovaro's rump, lifted Our Lady from

the ground, went up the steps, and pushed the heavy wooden door open. He set the figurine on the floor in front of the altar, then fumbled over the top of the altar until he found one of the candle holders. He lit the taper. The altar brightened. Our Lady's clam-shell housing seemed to gleam in anticipation of her return. Fargo stood looking at her for a long moment, again admiring her glittering adornments, the sparkle seeming to set her in motion.

"Lovely, wouldn't you agree?" Padre Bonelli's softly spoken words preceded him. The *padre* stepped from the bell-tower entrance and came to stand beside Fargo. Both men stared at Our Lady for a moment longer, neither speaking.

Fargo finally commented, "Gorgeous, in fact."

Padre Bonelli reached to touch the tiara. As the *padre* spoke, Fargo watched the man's fingers move excitedly over the diamonds. "Where did you find her? How did you get her back?"

"In Las Rocas. Not the town, but in the rocks. The how of it is not important. The villagers now have their statue back. That's what's counts, Padre."

Bonelli glanced to the open front door and back to Fargo before inquiring, "The woman? I have forgotten her name. Is she outside waiting for you? If so, may I ask her inside to share this moment with us?"

Fargo's head shook. "No, Padre, Marie Mercier is dead. Nobody waits outside." Even as he mouthed it, he wasn't quite sure it was true. A measure of doubt had crept into the tone of his voice at the end.

Padre Bonelli glanced sharply at him. "Are you saying somebody waits nearby? Outside the wall, perhaps?" He squatted and felt the ruby roses.

"All night, I had the feeling somebody was following me. But I was wrong. Nothing is out there that doesn't belong."

"You had reason to feel nervous, my friend. I know I would have been a tad concerned if—"

Fargo's brow furrowed when he heard the word "tad," and his quick verbal response interrupted the priest. "Tad? Did I hear you correctly? Tad? Who . . . what are you, anyhow?"

Before Fargo could draw his Colt, the man produced one just like it from his robe and pointed the weapon at Fargo's face. Rising from the squat, he said, "Frank Bonelli from New York City by way of Weatherford, Texas, and other places that wouldn't interest you. Use a thumb and forefinger to take the gun from its holster. Drop it to the floor. Move too fast and I'll shoot you here and now, a tad above the bridge of your nose."

After Fargo complied, the fellow kicked the Colt under the front-row pews and stepped back a few paces before continuing. "That's right, I'm not a priest. Catholic, yes, but not a man of the cloth.

"I murdered the priest the night before the Texicans rode in and took Our Lady, only hours before you arrived and sent those Apaches scurrying for cover. Strangled him, actually. Didn't want to be bothered with wiping up blood. I took the body out in the desert and left it for the buzzards.

"When dawn came, I told those who asked that God had called him away during the night, that he went fast to another place and left his blessings on everyone." Chuckling, he added, "They believed me until the Texicans stormed in. Then, after the savages retreated, I thought for a while these people might lynch me. Shit, I told them prayer would put everything back in order. Mister, I want you to know this is the most pious bunch of people I've ever seen."

Fargo glanced to Our Lady and grinned. "Well, Frank, she's back in town."

"That's right, but not for long. You said the tall brunette is dead. How'd she die?"

"A Mexican woman. You wouldn't know her. I have no idea why she shot Marie," Fargo lied.

Frank nodded slightly. "Just as well," he began. "I learned about her at the same time you did. Felix never told me he had a niece, and he sure as hell never told me he would be bringing a woman along."

"Uh, huh. Well, there's a lot of things Uncle Felix failed to mention."

"Such as?"

"He probably planned to kill us all after we had served his purposes. Chances are we would have departed this world at Guaymos after safe delivery of the statuette."

"You knew about Guaymos?"

"Felix told Marie. She told me and a room full of *bandidos*."

"Treacherous bastard. To think it was me who brought the deal to him. I had the merchandise—I guess I should say I knew where to steal it—and he had the connections in Europe, him being in the shipping business and all."

Since the moment Frank first revealed himself as a crook, Fargo had deduced he and Felix were in on it together. Now he thought back to Marie's sudden appearance and their subsequent dialogue, to search for a clue that would verify what Frank just said. He found it when he recalled Frank's expression when she told him her name. The expression, though fleeting, changed from curiosity to shock before he recovered.

Fargo needed time to think his way out of his predicament. He decided to enlighten the man a *bit*. "Marie Mercier was responsible for the gang of Texicans."

"Oh, I didn't know that. All this time I've been thinking they were Felix's henchmen. I thought they killed him and all those other people on that wagon train after Felix told them where they were going and why. So, that pretty bitch murdered her own uncle." Shaking his head, he continued. "You can't trust a woman. They'll betray you every time, every chance they get. Felix should have known better."

"That's why he brought her along," Fargo said to keep the conversation going.

"How's that?"

"For screwing."

"The hell you say. Sweet-looker like her? Maybe with you, perhaps, but her own kinfolk?"

"Hunh," Fargo snorted. "Her own and anybody else's."

Frank's free hand rose to his chin. Scratching it, he said, "Well, live and learn, I say. Felix never mentioned you, either. Hell, I needed some fast help. After seeing how you handled a gun when the Apaches attacked, I came looking for you first chance I got. Mass burials aren't my cup of tea. You might not believe me, but I intended to try to cut a deal with you when she butted in."

Fargo saw an opening. He squeezed into it, suggesting, "It's not too late to cut one with me," and heard it snap closed in his face.

"Nope. Good try, though. I don't need your gun now. By the crack of dawn, me and the little rich lady here, we'll be long gone."

"And me?"

"You? Hell, I ought to blow your brains out, but I won't. I think I'll leave you stranded here in Domingo long enough for me to get a good lead, put a lot of distance between us. Right now, I need your muscles. Pick her up and head for the door. That'll be my gun barrel you feel pressing on your back."

Once again Fargo clutched Our Lady to his chest, only this time he knew that behind the feel in the small of his back was a black hole surrounded by cold steel, and his death a quick trigger pull away.

Bonelli nudged him down the steps and told him to "tie her down on that mare." Fargo found this amusing but obeyed. Frank Bonelli wasn't near as good at what he was doing as he thought. Fargo had him pegged as a two-bit thief trying hard to act like an experienced robber, and the man simply didn't know how. Frank was careless. Frank let diamonds get in his eyes. Frank's mind, Fargo concluded, was somewhere else, probably in New York City, gambling with big shots, waltzing a fine filly around a ballroom floor, no telling what, but he damn sure wasn't concentrating on the work at hand. Fargo believed he could have knocked the Colt out of Frank's hand several times. He didn't, though, because he had a better, much safer idea.

Without Bonelli telling him to do it, Fargo got his throwing rope and connected the mare to the Ovaro with it, then held the pinto's bridle while Frank mounted up.

Frank had the Colt on him all the time, still did when he said, "All right, Mr. Fargo, now you can strip to raw skin and pitch your stuff up here to me. You'll find it somewhere out in the desert. Meantime, I want you walking around buck-naked." Chuckling, he explained, "There's nothing in this town that comes anywhere close to fitting you. Oh, I suppose you could wrap a dirty sheet around you." Bonelli motioned Fargo away from the stallion and to start undressing.

Fargo pulled off everything, including his throwing knife, which raised one of Bonelli's eyebrows when he saw it. When he retrieved his hat and put it on, Frank protested, but didn't shoot. After folding his clothes, Fargo tossed the bundle up to him.

Spurring the Ovaro to a walk, Frank said, "*Adiós,* my friend. Go to the cantina. The drinks are on me."

Fargo watched the thief and Our Lady leave the plaza and disappear around a corner, heading for the north gate. He went inside the mission and retrieved his Colt from under the pews. Turning toward the door, he whistled loudly. He moved behind the altar to wait for his stallion to come.

Drumming on top of the altar with his fingers, he listened to Bonelli hollering for the single-minded pinto to "whoa," then his shrieks of panic. "Goddammit, I said for you to whoa! Whoa, you big son of a bitch, whoa! Oh, shit, oh, shit. No! No, not that way! Whoa!"

When he heard the horses on the plaza in front of the mission, he knew the stallion was looking for its master. Fargo whistled again to give the horse an accurate bearing.

Frank was forced to hang on for dear life when the pinto, ears perked, leapt over the steps and plunged through the doorway with the mare trailing behind. The Ovaro trotted down the aisle and stopped in front of the altar. Frank stared at the dark hole aimed at him as Fargo squeezed the trigger.

The impact of the bullet knocked him back and off the horse. Fargo's clothing came unfolded as the bundle headed for the ceiling, peaked, and floated down to land behind the pinto. Frank's body tumbled on the floor and ended up sprawled between two rows of seats.

For the second time this night, Fargo removed Our Lady from the mare. This time he stood her on the pedestal in the housing, then he backed off the dais and considered her beauty for a moment. He winked and nodded his approval. Fargo pulled on his clothes, then led the two horses outside, where he again set the mare free.

He climbed into the saddle and took the big Ovaro to the shedlike stable. There he unsaddled it, removed all tack, watered and fed his horse, and inspected its hooves and shoes. Finding everything sound, he draped his saddlebags over a shoulder, picked up the Sharps, and went to pay Lupita a nocturnal visit.

He pushed her door open and looked inside the dark room. "Hey," he said, "wake up. You and I have unfinished business."

He heard her stir on the bed and ask sleepily, "Who is it?"

He stepped inside, tossed the saddlebags on the floor next to the door, and grunted, "Skye Fargo. You awake?"

"Fargo?" she cried. "But you're . . . Really?"

He heard the bed squeak an instant before her arms curled around his neck. She pressed hard against him. He wrapped an arm around her waist and lifted until their lips met. As they kissed openmouthed, he felt her slim legs wrap around his waist and the ankles lock to press firmly on his butt. She moaned, "I thought you were dead. Kiss me hard, Fargo, make me know it's really you. Oh, you taste so good."

He broke the mouth contact, but held her there. Squeezing her firm buttocks, he told her, "I'll taste better after a bath. What say you prepare one out back while I have a drink or two in the cantina? We'll make love till the sun comes up. Okay, *chiquita*?"

"*Sí.*" Her ankles released and he lowered her to the floor. She left, hurrying to comply with his wishes.

Fargo sauntered to the cantina. He paused in the doorway and raised a hand to his nape. The tiny hairs were standing straight out. Smoothing them down, he looked over his shoulder to maybe catch somebody staring at him. The street was as desolate as the desert. He shook off the annoying feeling, went behind the bar, got a bottle of bourbon and a glass, and took both to a table, where he sat facing the door. Peering out into the darkened street, he filled the glass and drank from it. His gun hand settled on the Colt's handle.

The bottle was half-empty when the back door grated open. Lupita announced his bath was ready. He took the bottle with him to the arbor. She had everything ready for him, including herself. She'd even remembered to place the little table next to the vat so his bottle, the soap, and washrag would be handy. He complimented her. She started undressing him, her busy fingers hastening to undo all the buttons they found. He sat on the edge of the tub and pulled off his boots, then stood to shuck his Levi's. Lupita preceded him into the water and sat with her back against one end of the shallow wood tub. When he stepped in and settled down, she giggled in anticipation.

"No fooling around," he said emphatically. "Right now all I want is to rid my body of the dunes of sand collected on it."

Reluctantly she sighed.

He permitted her to give his length a good scrubbing while he washed the rest of his body and drank the bottle empty.

They chatted while they scrubbed. The conversation drifted from the hot July weather, to how miserable she was being stuck in Domingo, back to the weather, and eventually to her sister.

"Did you see Chachona?" she inquired.

He frowned, for the question implied she knew her sister had gone to Las Rocas. "What makes you ask that?"

Lupita fumbled for an answer and finally blurted, "Uh, she rode south after you left. I know she wanted to follow you, so I thought—"

"She's dead," he interrupted.

Apparently his announcement stunned her. Her head bowed and he barely heard her mutter, "I told her El Jefe would kill her. I told her Lobo Loco had all the brains, but she wouldn't listen." She started to sob softly.

"El Jefe didn't kill your sister. A creature of the desert got her."

Surprised, her eyes flicked up. He nodded and continued. "A Gila monster bit her. It happened on our way back with Our Lady."

She reared back and gasped, almost shouting, "Our Lady? You got her back? She's here? In Domingo?"

"Yep. She's standing in her place, pretty as ever, waiting for the next priest to say Mass."

"*Next* priest? I don't understand."

"Well, I had to kill Father Bonelli. Poor man went crazy right before my eyes." He uncoiled and stepped out of the vat. Lupita came right behind him. He let her towel him dry.

The subject of Chachona, her death and relationship with El Jefe's *bandidos* was never brought up by either of them while drying off.

Lupita carried his clothes and led the way when they left the arbor. Passing through the cantina, he got a fresh bottle of bourbon.

After groping his way through her dark room to the bed, he found Lupita waiting for him on her hands and knees.

"Damn, honey." He chuckled while feeling over her trembling body. He knelt behind her and nudged her knees apart several inches wider. The head of his member felt her heat as he probed forward and slipped between the hot juicy lips. Holding it there, he took her by the hips and without further ado he pulled and shoved at the same time. She screamed, he went in to the hilt. The foreplay and preamble were over, now began the pleasure-filled contest of who could wear out the other first.

The small room soon became filled with her shrieks and screams. Their grunts and groans seemed like those made by wounded soldiers. Lupita's moans and sighs could have been the victorious general's, her gasps of delight mirrored brave soldiers' astonishments of first successes in the heat of hand-to-hand combat. Fargo thrust into her time and time again, while she tried to capture him in a slickened tunnel that squeezed and released, squeezed anew. The tiny battlefield grew quite hot.

Their pleasure went on and on, without letting up, until the bed was soaked with sweat. Then she laid her quivering, fully satisfied nakedness on his muscled, glistening torso and rested her head in the crook of his right shoulder. Both quickly found sleep.

Fargo's eyes flicked open. That he could now vaguely see the ceiling and the corners where it met the wall, told him the door was open. Dawn's first stage of breaking light crept inside.

He turned his head, expecting to see Lupita asleep beside him, and found her gone. Thinking she had left to go prepare their breakfast and would be back momentarily, he took his time pulling on his clothes. As he did, he felt the hairs on the back of his neck tingle.

Glancing through the doorway, he reached down for his gun belt. When his hand didn't touch it, he fumbled for it under the bed. A surge of concern swept through him when the searching hand didn't find the gun belt.

He stood and felt all over the floor with his feet, but the gun belt wasn't there. The saddlebags lay where he'd dropped them, but his Sharps no longer stood at the wall next to them. He left the saddlebags where they lay and went outside.

Looking into the north sky, he noted the Big Dipper's position put the hour at about six o'clock. Somewhere on the far side of Domingo a cock crowed. Fargo glanced toward the cantina, but started walking toward the plaza. He stayed in the blackness that still covered the east side of the street.

At the corner, he halted and flattened his back to the wall. His gaze focused on the small group of people watering their horses at the well. The people and horses were too bunched up for him to distinguish how many formed the group or who they were.

Fargo's wild-creature hearing easily picked up their conversation. He separated six voices, Lupita's when she laughed, and five of El Jefe's *bandidos*. There was no mistaking Lobo Loco's guttural tone. He believed the others were Vergón, El Ratón, Cabrón, and Feo.

He watched them spread the horses apart. A donkey rigged for packing stood in the clearing. As he watched, Our Lady was put on the animal and lashed down. While their attention was centered on the statuette, Fargo eased around the corner and hugged the wall as he moved to get into position to dash across the clearing and go to the mission. Speed was essential, the breaking light his enemy.

He took a deep breath, checked the group a final time, saw most still had their backs to him, then ran in a crouch to the mission's south wall. Peeking around the corner, he saw them assembled as before, still talking, tying down Our Lady. From this angle he saw the donkey's side. The donkey had not yet been rigged to trail. Fargo had to get inside the mission.

He hurried to the rear and tried the back door. He shoved hard on it twice, but it wouldn't budge. He moved to a window, but it was locked. The next one opened up about an inch, then froze tight. The fingers on both hands worked into the scant crack. He heaved upward with all his strength. The window raised slowly, reluctantly, and with noisy rebellion. Fargo shoved up on it harder, and when the lower part cleared the bind, it slid up easily.

He stuck a leg inside and rolled through to stand in the room. Moving swiftly, he went to the sanctuary and found Bonelli's body still sprawled on the floor.

Dropping to hands and knees, he searched the floor around the dead man to find Frank's Colt. Not finding it, he believed the *bandidos* had; he stood, reached down, and grabbed a fistful of Bonelli's robe and snatched him angrily out into the aisle. The Colt lay on the floor where the man's chest had been. Fargo picked up the gun.

He stood just inside the doorway and looked at the six men huddled in a loose group not fifty feet away. He could not waste one bullet.

Lupita held his Sharps. His gun belt with his Colt holstered hung on Lobo Loco's hips. Fargo desperately needed one of those weapons, or one of theirs, although he didn't fancy French-made shooting irons.

Staring at the tight cluster of *bandidos*, he reasoned that his best chance for success would be to disburse them. If he shot from the doorway, he could drop one, maybe two before the others threw down on him and sent a fusillade of slugs tearing in at him. He couldn't take the risk of one of the bullets finding him.

He cocked the hammer, then backed down the aisle ten paces, got set, and ran as hard and fast as he could move through the doorway. He leapt over the steps and hit the ground running. Halfway to them, he shot Vergón in the head. Before he could squeeze off another round, the men scattered like a covey of quail leaving a pile of brush.

Lobo Loco sprinted right for the road leading out of the village to the north. Feo got behind a skittish horse, while El Ratón ran like the wind in the direction of the cantina. Lupita, he noticed, ducked behind the well.

He shot El Ratón square in the back. He stumbled crazily and fell facedown in the dirt. The horses panicked, reared, and ran from the big man wielding the big gun.

Exposed, Feo made an easy target. Fargo's bullet

tore off the left side of the ugly man's face. He dropped in his tracks, dead before hitting the ground.

Both Lobo Loco and Lupita shot at him. Two of the bullets swished close by his head and thudded into the front wall of the mission. The third bullet hit the ground between his feet.

"You're next, Lupita," Fargo shouted.

As she leveled the Sharps on the edge of the well, he dived to the ground and crabbed against the other side of it. A quick glance around the curve of the well showed Lobo Loco had that side covered from where he was hunkered in the doorway of a dwelling. "They've thrown you to the buzzards, honey," Fargo needled. "Better give up or I'll have to shoot you."

The Sharps barked. A chunk flew out of the top of the well's rim above his head. Fargo inched his way around the south side of the well until Lupita came partly in view. She was kneeling with the Sharps barrel still on the top edge of the well. He pushed forward and rolled onto his back at the same time. The gun hand and the Colt gripped in it automatically extended toward her. "Don't," he warned. She swung the Sharps down to shoot him. Fargo's shot tore through her head. He grabbed the Sharps and loaded it.

"Hey, Lobo! I know where you are! There's only the one way out. You can't stay there forever. You want to talk, or shoot it out with me? Your choice, *amigo*, but make it snappy because I've got an appointment to keep in a few minutes."

Lobo Loco was easier than Fargo imagined. "*Sí*, I will shoot it out with you. I will kill you with your own gun."

"*Muy bien*," Fargo replied. "You count to three and step out in the open, and I'll step away from the well. Cheat, and I'll come strangle the life out of you."

He knelt when he heard *uno*, crouched on *dos*, and

leapt out on *tres*. Not only was Lobo Loco outside, he'd taken advantage of the slow count and moved halfway to the corner.

They fired simultaneously, both missing due to the unexpected positions of their targets. Running for the corner, Lobo Loco fired a second shot, which also went wild.

As the *bandido* swung around the corner, Fargo raised the Sharps and shot from the hip. Lobo Loco's momentum, compounded by the slug that tore into his shoulder, carried him out into the street where he tried to turn and shoot. Fargo fired the last bullet in Frank's Colt into the man's brain.

Two roosters crowing broke the silence in Domingo.

He went to Feo, got his knife, and transferred the sheath from the dead man's calf to his own. From Lobo Loco he got his Colt and gun belt. While strapping on the gun belt, he noticed several doors in the abodes were partly open and eyeballs peered through the cracks.

"Don't be afraid, *amigos*," he told them. "You can come out. It's all over." He hoped it was true.

He headed toward the well but stopped and turned back when a young voice behind him asked, "Our Lady?"

People were coming outside cautiously, glancing up and down the street to make sure it was safe, ready to flee back inside if things didn't look right. The young boy approached with a questioning expression on his face. "She's around," Fargo answered. "Riding a donkey." He shot the youngster a wink.

The unexpected disclosure spawned murmurs from the crowd that had formed in the street. Looking down at Lobo Loco's twisted body, Fargo explained, "This man and several others took her from the mission. They were tying Our Lady on a pack donkey when I woke up and saw what was happening. You people have six fresh bodies to bury. Come on, we'll go find the donkey and return the statue to the church."

They surged past him to begin the search and call the other villagers out to help, assuring them it was safe. Fargo glanced about the plaza and didn't see the donkey. They'll find it quick enough, he told himself. He went to the well and hauled up a bucket of water. After drinking from it, he poured the rest on top of his head. He sat on the edge of the well to wait and to help them tote the statue inside the mission.

As the people started drifting back to the well, the morning sun peeked over the east wall and its rays sliced across the plaza from either side of the mission. They came shaking their heads to those already assembled around it, and after joining them, they discussed things in low tones.

An older man, gaunt of face, slim as a rail, and with hair white as snow, took charge. Bracing himself on a gnarled wood cane, he spoke Spanish in a loud raspy voice, asking, "You, Carlos Maldonado, did you think to look over the south wall?" Carlos' head shook. "Humph," the old man snorted, and cut his watery eyes to another man. "Did you look everywhere?"

"Yes, Manuel, everywhere," the man replied. "Even in all the homes. Our Lady is not in the east side of Domingo."

Manuel's eyes darted to a fat woman. "Eh, Dolores?"

"No," she answered. "The donkey did not go west. We searched everywhere." Glancing to a young man, she sought verification. "Is that not right?"

The young man nodded. Manuel's attention shifted to a man slightly younger than himself but equally as thin. The man simply shook his head.

"Humph," the old man repeated, and looked at Fargo. "What do you think, *señor*? There is no place in Domingo for a donkey to hide."

"I agree," Fargo answered. "Did any of you think to look inside the mission?"

"Yes," two women chorused. One deferred to the other, who added, "We looked in all the rooms. The donkey is not there. Neither is Our Lady. We found our *padre's* body, though."

Fargo wanted to tell them Frank wasn't a priest, but it would only confuse an already baffling situation more. He suggested, "You people need to send a messenger to the bishop to report on things and ask him to send a replacement for Father Bonelli." That will shake the diocese, he thought. "Don't worry about the donkey or Our Lady," he told the crowd. "Donkeys can get in the damnedest places, usually where you least expect. It'll show up."

Most all nodded in agreement. He noticed twin young women smiling broadly. He wasn't sure if he saw happiness or lust in their eyes. Both were unusually pretty, still slim, almost willowy.

A female voice spoke from the outer rim of the circle and took his gaze away from the winsome pair. "This may be a sign from God that we do not deserve having Our Lady. Maybe our faith—"

The old man, stiffening erect and cutting his eyes sharply at her, broke the forming implication of lack of faith. Pointing the tip of his cane toward her, he surprised Fargo and most of the others, saying, "You are correct, Elena Suárez. Only God can make things disappear. God gives and God takes away." The pointing cane swung before their faces as he turned full circle, saying, "We are alive because of this man. Be grateful. Pray on it. Show this brave man we can be happy even in bad times."

"Fiesta?" a man shouted rather hopefully.

The old man aimed his cane at him, smiled, and said, "Yes. Good thinking, Pablo." Lowering the cane, he said to all, "We give a *fiesta* to honor this man."

No orders for the distribution of the workload were necessary. Each person knew what they were to do. Within seconds Skye Fargo found himself alone at the well. He grinned, pushed away, and headed for the shed to check on his horse.

On the way, he went in the cantina to have a drink or two of bourbon. A chubby fellow stooped behind the bar, where he'd already put six unopened bottles. As Fargo watched, the fellow's hands appeared and set two more on the bar. Fargo opened a bottle of bourbon and swilled from it. Two more bottles came up.

Fargo rested his back against the bar and looked out into the street, now bustling with villagers carrying things for the fiesta on the *zócalo*. The back door squeaked open. His head swung around and his gun hand went to the Colt. He relaxed and lowered the hand when he saw one of the twins standing in the doorway, smiling big, batting her eyelashes at him. He shook his head and moved for the front door.

Inside the shed the pinto was taking advantage of the shade and still-cool morning air by having a well-earned nap. His head snapped up and the horse looked around at Fargo. Before the Ovaro could stand, Fargo coaxed the stallion to stay down. All he wanted was to see if the pinto was still there and unharmed by Lobo Loco and his gang. He squatted and rubbed the Ovaro's forehead and his powerful neck before rising to leave.

A xylophonist accompanied by a coronet player provided the music for the *fiesta*. Most everyone hummed along with them. Fargo gnawed on a leg of lamb, watching a fast-footed lean handsome man do the Mexican hat dance around the wide brim of a large *sombrero* somebody tossed to the ground. Everyone was happy. For the moment the ordeals at Domingo were forgotten. They were swept up in the thrill of the party.

As two-o'clock siesta time approached, the crowd began to thin. Fargo sat on the mission's steps and eyed one of the twins. She promenaded before him numerous times, using her dark eyes and full lips to flirt provocatively. A hefty lady with a scowl on her face came and grabbed the young girl by an arm. Leading her away, the woman admonished her severely for such a brazen display.

Much later, only Fargo and the two musicians were left on the plaza. He listened to them play a slow and soft tune that he didn't recognize, then they too departed to take a nap. Fargo stood, stretched, and walked to get his horse. He walked the pinto to the cantina and went inside to fetch a fresh bottle for the trail. The *fiesta* had claimed all but a near-empty bottle of tequila, which he took. Then he led the stallion to Lupita's door, reached inside for his saddlebags, and draped them on the horse. Before mounting, he retrieved from the left bag the money he'd found in Marie's secret compartment in her saddlebags.

Riding to the mission, he counted off the amount he felt was due him. He left the rest on Our Lady's pedestal for the villagers to find and maybe wonder if God was not indeed benevolent.

Coming outside, he heard a donkey bray. The sound came from behind the mission. He rode around to investigate, but it wasn't the same donkey. He turned the Ovaro and headed for the north gateway.

As he rode north across the desert, a fiercely hot sun blazed down on him. Late in the afternoon the shimmering waves of heat began to dissipate. They vanished altogether shortly before the sun lowered to the horizon. At sunset he halted and watched the fiery red arc sink from sight while he tipped the mouth of his canteen to the pinto's waiting tongue and sloshed on some of the precious water. He took one small swallow when he was back in the saddle.

Much later, he saw the massacre site ahead of him. Coming closer, he saw the wagons had been turned over where they last stood in a defensive circle. He rode between two and dismounted in the center of the circle.

As his gaze moved from one wagon to another, he could only imagine the shocked surprise of the Apaches when they saw the big Conestogas looming dead ahead in their path of flight after their defeat at Domingo.

When he thought about the savages racing in with vengeance in their eyes and war whoops, only to find the people dead, a belly chuckle escaped through his lips. Frustrated by being denied a second chance to kill and unable to slaughter already dead whites, they pushed the wagons over and went home, there to lie and brag about a tough battle that was never fought.

Fargo checked the water barrels. Only one still held water. He let the Ovaro drink first.

While tipping the rim of the barrel to drink what the pinto left, the hair on the back of Fargo's neck rose. He dropped the barrel, drew his Colt, and spun to shoot.

The donkey with Our Lady on its back stood in the center of the circle.

He picked up the barrel and took it to the donkey. While he tested Our Lady's bindings, the donkey slurped the remaining water. An odd thought came into Fargo's mind.

He searched the overturned wagons until he found the top hat Marie had mentioned. Felix's rotting remains lay in the downside corner of the Conestoga. He left the body there and took the top hat to the donkey, stopping to pick up a shovel on the way.

After digging a grave in the center of the circle of wagons, he tossed in the hat, then went to the donkey and began relieving it of its glorious one-of-a-kind burden.

Fargo stepped down into the grave and gently laid Our Lady on the bottom. He covered her face with the top hat so she wouldn't see.

Ten minutes later he tossed on the last shovel of desert sand, patted it smooth with the instrument, then stood back. Feeling he should say something profound, he removed his hat. When he opened his mouth to speak, his tongue locked up on him.

During the sudden attack of lockjaw, he remembered the old man with the cane had said the disappearance of the donkey and Our Lady might be a sign from God. In that moment two things happened simultaneously and ended his gaping: several brilliant shooting stars streaked downward in the inky sky, and the donkey brayed.

He put his hat on and went to the magnificent shiny black-and-white stallion. He eased up into the saddle and rode from the circle without looking back. After a spell, his hand dipped into his pocket and the fingers touched Marie's compact.

Fondling the compact, Fargo muttered, "Maybe Miss Candy will want it."

The tingle of hairs springing up on his nape shattered his vision of Miss Candy lying in bed. As a frown formed on his face, he thought he heard a coyote howling from afar. Shifting in the saddle, he stared into the black night toward Las Rocas. He muttered dryly, "Skye Fargo, you have to quit imagining things. You didn't hear that damn coyote."

Fargo rode on.

LOOKING FORWARD!
The following is the opening
section from the next novel in the exciting
Trailsman series from Signet:
THE TRAILSMAN #99
CAMP ST. LUCIFER

*Summer, 1860, it began and ended in Colorado,
during a raging storm, on a muddy street,
where the devil's worst were gathered
and sent back to hell . . .*

Shortly after the big man cleared Raton Pass at mid-morning, the leading edge of dark, roiling clouds burst over the breathtaking Sangre de Cristo Range and passed low over the trail. Behind him stretched the vast, desolate New Mexico Territory, raw and un-tamed. Somewhere ahead was Walsenburg, his imme-diate destination.

Within minutes a sprinkle of huge raindrops dim-pled the dry, soft soil around him. He dismounted and drew his rain slicker out of the bedroll.

Hours later, though the ugly, nearly black overcast had not unleashed lightning or thunder, the deluge continued unceasingly. The slicker offered precious little relief as a cold, wind-driven rain lashed the big man and the Ovaro on which he rode. The stallion's jet-black fore and hindquarters and white midsection glistened.

At dusk the pinto's ears perked and swiveled for-ward. Skye Fargo glanced up from the stream of muddy water he'd been watching course through the low spots on the winding trail. On his right were several dead, gnarled black oak trees, their big, barren branches reaching toward him, not unlike an old hag's. On more than one trunk he saw the rain and dusky shadows seemed to cast as devil's faces staring out at him.

Moments later, the vague shape of a low structure loomed out of the densely falling rain. Normally a weather-beaten gray, the wide boards of the walls were now dark, almost black, dulled by the steady falling rain. The gloomy building's roof slanted back at a sharp angle. A sheet of water seemed to leap from the low side of the roof and had formed its own tributary, also rushing south. A black rectangle high enough to accommodate a mounted rider identified itself as the front entrance.

The trail quickly widened into a street. Fargo rode down its middle and past the low structure on his right, which he now recognized as a smithy. On his left was a small building. The rain-drenched sign on its front identified it as a land office. On his right another sign painted above the door of a somewhat larger buildings read "PEARSON'S FIREARMS." No lamps burned inside either edifice, but ahead, light spilled through windows in buildings on both sides of the street. A long line of saddled horses stood at hitching rails in front of the two-story structure on his left. The sound of piano music filtered out. Another stream of light came from what was clearly a small café.

Adjacent to the café stood a large two-story building. A slim man stood on its long front porch, his back to the front door. Fargo angled toward the man. Coming closer, he saw tall white letters that spelled "BUCKHORN HOTEL" on the wall over the porch. He reined the Ovaro to a halt facing the man, who he now saw was no more than forty and had a receding hairline and a thin nose. He was intently watching the stream of mud, as though it might change course any second, spill over the porch, and come inside the hotel.

Fargo cleared his throat loudly. The man glanced up at him. Fargo said, "Evening, mister. I'm looking for the public stable."

The man pointed to the far corner. "It's on Dynamite Street, down aways on the right, next to the wagon repair. Can't miss it. Follow your nose. The stable's stink will take you straight to it."

Fargo nodded and reined the pinto that way. The Buckhorn Hotel set on the southeast corner of the intersection. Directly across from it was a barber shop. On the northeast corner stood a huge feed store, and directly across from it, on the northwest corner, was a bank. Fargo rounded the corner occupied by the barber shop. Wall-mounted lamps burned inside.

An unusually wide wagon-repair place was behind the bank. Across the street from the wagon repair and next to a sheltered, high board fence behind the barber shop was a spacious corral holding at least a dozen horses. The vague shape of the stable slowly emerged in the downpour.

Rain-blurred glimmers of lantern light reflected yellow on the wet ground in the middle of the dark front opening. The strong scent of horse manure and hay emanated from the building.

As Fargo punched through the torrential downpour he saw a barrel-chested older man with a gray beard and bushy moustache, both stained with visible evidence of chewing tobacco. He stood in the wide opening of the tall frame structure, the lantern at his feet. His hands were jammed so far down in his pockets that the red suspenders holding up the pants were tight as banjo strings and grooving his shoulders. He was studying the swift-running stream of muddy water churning down the street, dangerously close to his business.

He lifted his studious gaze when the Ovaro walked up and Fargo reined it to a halt. "Whut'cha want?" the man asked in a gruff, no-nonsense tone, quickly adding, "Drifters usually hitch their horses out front of the saloon."

"I'm no drifter, old man. Got an empty stall for the night?"

"Mebbe." He cocked his head and squinted up at Fargo's chiseled face. "Have to see money first." He spat a long brown stream toward the mud flow.

Fargo understood his concern. You could count on drifters to take advantage of good-natured people. He flipped a silver dollar to him. The old man bit it to make sure it was real, then said, "Welcome, stranger." As he pocketed the coin, a dry grin rearranged his moustache. "Mite wet, ain't it? Ride on in."

He stepped back and led the way. A half-dozen horses were tethered to rungs on the boards at the far end of the alleyway separating the stalls on either side. "Cowpokes' animals," the old man explained over his shoulder. "Some like to put their horses inside. I tether 'em for two bits overnight. That way they get to piss the other six bits off gambling." His head shook solemnly. Swinging a stall gate open, he said, "Only one left. You're lucky, friend."

Fargo dismounted and stripped the Ovaro. The old man handed him a wad of rags. Fargo began drying off the stallion.

"Mighty fine pinto you have there," the man offered. "Wouldn't want to sell him, would you?"

"Not for sale." Fargo reached inside his saddlebags and brought out a dandy brush, which he used to remove several lumps of mud from the stallion's coat. Satisfied, he returned the dandy brush and brought out the hoof pick. He started cleaning the horse's left front hoof first.

A horse and rider came through the entrance. Three others quickly followed. Fargo glanced their way. None wore slickers, but all wore gun belts. As they dismounted, the old man hurried to them.

Fargo kept cleaning the Ovaro's hooves and checking the shoes, but he was alert to the conversation at the entrance. The old man was saying quite emphatically, "Private stalls? I ain't got any left. Ain't got no place to put your animals. I'm full up for the night."

"Well, you old fool, empty four," the hard voice of the bigger man ordered. "Hitch 'em outside in the rain if you have to, but we're coming in."

"Oh, you are, huh?" The old man's tone carried a fight in it. He tested the new arrivals. "I suppose you're prepared to pay double *and* face the owners of the horses when they come for them in the morning and I tell what happened."

"Naw, old man," the bigger man snorted, "we ain't paying double. We ain't paying nothing. Anybody wants to make something out of it, he'll get hurt. We came to see Thurston, so get them four stall ready."

Fargo lowered the stallion's left rear hoof to the ground. He moved through the heavy shadows next to the stalls and came up behind the husky man giving the stable owner a hard time.

"Thurston?" the old man cried, his voice now definitely angry. "Get outta my place, you sonsabitches! I don't stable drifters! 'Specially those friendly with that bastard!"

"Pete, go clean out four stalls," the bigger man growled.

As the old man stood his ground, saying, "You do and—!" Fargo's left forearm clamped tight around the bigger man's throat. Before the men could react and go for their guns, Fargo slapped the Colt upside the head of the man he held.

When he brought his powerful forearm away, the man's knees buckled and he sunk to the ground. Fargo swung the Colt to aim gut-level from one to the other of the three men while hissing, "Get him on his horse and get out of here. The old man said he doesn't want your business."

Fargo watched as they obeyed him. He ingrained the images of their faces in his mind. The one he had knocked to his knees had a cruel scar across his chin and deep-sunken eyes that held hate.

The shortest man had a wide nose and dark eyes that were in constant motion.

The other two men were both about six feet tall. One was lantern-jawed, the other had a short red beard sprinkled with black hairs.

The old man was wrong. They were a notch above common drifters. Drifting, yes, but these men would murder to get what they wanted . . . and rape and plunder. Alone, none had the backbone to do it. But as a group they could intimidate. All four were the kind who would kill their own mothers for a nickel. Men like these, ignorant and uncaring, were highly dangerous, especially in dark places. They bore watching.

"I'll get you for this," the hurt man snarled from his mounted position in his saddle. He held a palm to the side of his face and stared coldly at Fargo as they rode out.

"I'll be around," Fargo answered.

The old man booted a horse apple through the opening. "What did you butt in for?" he complained bitterly. "I coulda took care of them rotten sonsabitches all by myself."

Fargo grinned slightly and cocked his head to one side. "Sorry. I guess I underestimated you."

The old man grumbled under his breath while he followed Fargo back to the Ovaro. Fargo nudged the horse inside the stall and said, "Give him good oats and hay, plenty of water. I'll be back at dawn."

"Even if it's still gully-washing like this?" The old man's expression conveyed more concern than did his tone of voice.

Fargo closed and secured the gate. "We're used to it," he replied dryly. "Who runs the hotel?"

"Ben Voss and his wife, Freida, they own it. You'll find the Buckhorn right across from that no-good Douglas Thurston's new Saloon and Gambling Emporium." He paused, then grunted, "Highway Robbery Emporium if you ask me."

Fargo leaned against the gate and rested a boot on the bottom slat. "Oh? What do you mean by that? Are you saying this man Thurston cheats?"

The old man scratched his beard. "Don't rightly know, mister. Let's say ain't nobody caught him at it. But there ain't a man alive who has that much good luck. Leastwise I ain't never met such a man . . . till Douglas Thurston came to Walsenburg 'bout six months ago, that is."

"What does your sheriff have to say about it?"

The old man scowled, "Hunh. Thurston had Howard an' his deputy, Earl Davidson, shot dead first thing after he came to town. Right in front of the saloon. Two cowards did it for him. Didn't see it myself. Folks who did said they was devils. One was only half a man—a dreadful sight I'm told—an' the other had a long scar on his face." The old man drug a fingernail down the left side of his face. "The sons-abitches shot 'em in the back. We ain't got no sheriff. Everybody's afraid to wear the badge."

The saddlebags were draped over his shoulder and the Sharps in his hand. Fargo headed for the opening, commenting, "Maybe Thurston isn't all that lucky."

The old man hurried to catch up. He snorted, "Whaddaya mean by that?"

"Maybe the rest of you give him his good luck."

"How's that?" He tugged Fargo's shirt sleeve to make him wait and explain before stepping out in the rain.

"While many sit to gamble, few know how. Where do I get a hot bath?"

"Fred Hushour's barber shop is next door to the saloon. Fred, he can fix you up with a bath for a nickel. Whaddaya mean, 'few know how'?"

"Just what I said." Fargo glanced at the black sky, then stepped out in the rain and mud.

Behind him the old man grumbled, "Dammit, mister, come back here and tell me what you meant by that. You . . ." His voice trailed off, absorbed by the rain.

At the Buckthorn the man on the porch smiled and shook his head when Fargo walked up and joined him.

"You Ben Voss?"

"Yes, sir."

"Got a room for the night?"

"Eight, in fact. But that will change in a few hours." Voss's eyes cut past Fargo to the saloon.

Fargo looked at the noisy establishment barely visible through the hard, steady rainfall. "How long does that racket go on?"

"Until all the suckers go home flat broke . . . or pass out."

Fargo chuckled. "That old man at the livery said much the same. Sounds like you people have a problem."

"Neil Kaspar? Well, he ought to know. Thurston's took just about all Neil owns. All he has left is the livery, and Thurston will have it by the end of the month."

"If you have one, give me an upstairs back room where I won't have to listen to that noise all night."

Ben ushered him into a small, clean lobby dominated by a splendid rack of elkhorns displayed on the wall directly above the lower steps of a narrow staircase. A long mirror hung on the wall across from where a chubby, thin-lipped woman dressed in black and light brown gingham stood behind the registration counter. Room keys hung from pegs inches from her back, and an open ledger lay on the counter before her.

Ben asked her to put their guest in number 9. She turned the ledger for Fargo to sign.

Fargo touched the brim of his soggy hat. "Evening, Mrs. Voss."

The schoolmarm bun coiled on her head nodded slightly. She glanced down to watch him enter his name. "Staying long, Mr. Fargo?" Freida Voss obviously knew how to read upside down. Most teachers could. Fargo bet the serious-faced woman wielded a mean schoolroom paddle too.

"Be leaving at the crack of dawn, ma'am."

She handed him the room key. "That will be one dollar, Mr. Fargo. The stairs to the privy out back are at the end of the hall." When she next spoke, Fargo detected a look in her eyes that might have said I-don't-like-doing-it-but-we're-broke. "If you wish, I'll be more than happy to wash and iron your clothes tonight. Ben will bring them to you in the morning when you wake up. Just stomp the floor several times when you're ready. Our bedroom is below yours. Washing and ironing is twenty-five cents."

Fargo paid her. "I'll stomp on the floor when they're ready to come down to you."

"Yes, sir. Thank you for staying at the Buckhorn."

Fargo stayed in his room long enough to drop off his saddlebags and Sharps, then went next door to the café.

Two tables with red-and-white-striped tablecloths stood next to the front windows. A row of eight free-standing wooden stools were neatly spaced in a line in front of a counter dotted with salt and pepper shakers and shotglasses filled with flat toothpicks. All wall surfaces were white and looked as though they'd been freshly painted. Fargo took a stool left of center in the row.

A rotund man older than Neil Kaspar stood behind the counter, staring blankly through the rain-drenched windows. Fargo didn't know whether the fixation was on the ever-widening current of muddy water or the saloon beyond it. Puffy coffee-hued bags bulged under the man's glazed dark eyes, deep set in his clean shaven beefy face.

Fargo interrupted the man's stolid gaze, saying, "Biggest steak you have. While it's cooking, keep filling a cup with hot coffee."

The man blinked, stiffened, and shouted toward an archway on his left, "Burn a steer, Millie!" He set a cup and saucer before his customer.

A young, rather attractive female poked her head and shoulders through the opening. Dark blue eyes batted above her nice smile as she looked at Fargo.

Without looking at her, the man snapped, "Stop ogling the customers and do what I said." He turned and filled the cup with steaming brew, mumbling, "Young wives are more problems than they're worth."

Fargo swiveled around to face the saloon while he sipped from the cup. A lean man about five feet ten pushed through the saloon's swinging doors and paused under the porch's overhanging roof to raise his collar and hunch his shoulders. He dashed out into the rain, leaped the mud-swollen surge, and burst through the café door, laughing. The older man's sullen expression underwent a dramatic change. Now his eyes seemed to twinkle.

Before the beaming youth—Fargo put him at twenty—sat three stools down from him, near the open archway, Fargo noticed the youngster's big belt buckle was in the shape of Texas. He also wore a gun belt fashioned from black leather, dressed with care; water beaded on it rather than soaked in. The holster rode low on his left thigh and was held down by a black leather thong. The holster held a Smith & Wesson with ivory grips.

He said cheerily, "Evening, Mr. Wilson." Leaning toward the opening, he added, "You too, Mrs. Wilson."

Mr. Wilson replied, "Evening, kid. Winning or losing?"

"Losing," Millie's lilting voice answered from the kitchen. "Howdy, kid. What can I fix for my sweetie?"

"Aw, shucks, ma'am, same as always, I reckon." Fargo thought he saw a hint of a blush spread across the kid's face when she called him sweetie. When Mr. Wilson set a cup and saucer on the counter and began filling it, the young cowboy drawled, "That Thurston's the luckiest devil this side of the Pecos."

Wilson's eyes darted at the rain-slickened window as he scowled, "Yeah, well, if the sonofabitch lays his nasty eyes on Millie's ass again, I'll send him to hell and let him try double-dealing Satan."

He'd spoken loud enough for her to hear. She changed the subject. "Found your man yet, kid?"

The kid swallowed some of his coffee first. "No, ma'am, but he'll come this way sooner or later. I can't go riding all over to find the man, even though Mr. Hollis said for me to. I'll just stay put a while longer and wait for him to come along."

Fargo looked at him and said, "I see you're from Texas."

"Yes, sir. Estelline."

"Ranch hand?"

"Yes, sir. I work for Mr. Richard Hollis, owner of the Bar Z Bar spread. I'm not much at dogging steers, though." Fargo saw the blush form again. The wrangler added, "But I make up for it in other ways."

Fargo bet he did indeed. He suspected the young man would be a deadly accurate shot and fast as a striking rattler. His gaze lowered to the Smith & Wesson, slowly so the kid would notice.

The kid cut an easy grin that would put most folks at ease. Fargo had seen the same disarming grin in his own mirror many times. Behind the kid's grin was instant justice. Fargo wondered if the lazy, upturned corners of the lips remained while the cowboy meted out his brand of swift comeuppance with the Smith & Wesson. Some law-and-order men's did, others did not.

"How's it going over at the Emporium?" Fargo nodded toward the saloon.

The kid blossomed a nice smile that presented even white teeth. "Packed house," he replied. "Only two fistfights so far this evening. The piano music is pretty good, though. No pianos in Estelline. Mostly I go there to watch and listen while I wait."

Fargo was ready to believe that the pleasant young ranch hand and himself were the only ones in town who weren't victims of the Emporium. He didn't pry for the wait-for-who. The kid had already mentioned *the* man would come along sooner or later. It sounded as though he meant a drifter or outlaw, one who would get to see the easy grin.

A thick, juicy steak that overlapped the ends of the platter was placed in front of Fargo and brought an end to the budding conversation.

Before taking her hands away from the platter, Millie stared and smiled at her big customer, too long for her husband. He nudged her aside and handed Fargo a carving knife, then turned his attention back to the sandy-haired cowpuncher. Millie swelled up in a huff and walked back to her kitchen.

Fargo watched her rolling rump, knowing her husband had a greater problem than he probably imagined, and the man probably imagined much.

Fargo ate, settled up with Wilson, and stood to leave. At the door he heard the sound of a shot pierce the downpour. His right hand automatically gripped the handle of his Colt.

Just before it did, he heard the Smith & Wesson's hammer cock behind him.

LIFE ON THE FRONTIER

☐ **THE OCTOPUS by Frank Norris.** Rippling miles of grain in the San Joaquin Valley in California are the prize in a titanic struggle between the powerful farmers who grow the wheat and the railroad monopoly that controls its transportation. As the struggle flourishes it yields a grim harvest of death and disillusion, financial and moral ruin. "One of the few American novels to bring a significant episode from our history to life."—Robert Spiller (517113—$3.50)

☐ **THE OUTCASTS OF POKER FLAT and Other Tales by Bret Harte.** Stories of 19th century Far West and the glorious fringe-inhabitants of Gold Rush California. Introduction by Wallace Stegner, Stanford University. (523466—$4.50)

☐ **THE CALL OF THE WILD and Selected Stories by Jack London.** Foreword by Franklin Walker. The American author's vivid picture of the wild life of a dog and a man in the Alaska gold fields. (523903—$2.50)

☐ **LAUGHING BOY by Oliver LaFarge.** The greatest novel yet written about the American Indian, this Pulitzer-prize winner has not been available in paperback for many years. It is, quite simply, the love story of Laughing Boy and Slim Girl—a beautifully written, poignant, moving account of an Indian marriage. (522443—$3.50)

☐ **THE DEERSLAYER by James Fenimore Cooper.** The classic frontier saga of an idealistic youth, raised among the Indians, who emerges to face life with a nobility as pure and proud as the wilderness whose fierce beauty and freedom have claimed his heart. (516451—$2.95)

☐ **THE OX-BOW INCIDENT by Walter Van Tilburg Clark.** A relentlessly honest novel of violence and quick justice in the Old West. Afterword by Walter Prescott Webb. (523865—$3.95)

Prices slightly higher in Canada.

Buy them at your local bookstore or use this convenient coupon for ordering.

NEW AMERICAN LIBRARY
P.O. Box 999, Bergenfield, New Jersey 07621

Please send me the books I have checked above. I am enclosing $_____ (please add $1.00 to this order to cover postage and handling). Send check or money order—no cash or C.O.D.'s. Prices and numbers are subject to change without notice.

Name_____

Address_____

City _____ State _____ Zip Code _____
Allow 4-6 weeks for delivery.
This offer, prices and numbers are subject to change without notice.